More Than Ivory

Gina Augustini Best

For those still missing, taken against their will, and for the families who continue to search for them.

CHAPTER I

Three Days Missing

To anyone watching from a distance, I'm sure we looked like a parade of the blind. Truth is, we were blind. Not to mention, desperate. That was my mood, anyway, as we combed the area for scraps of clothing or a glint of metal, or anything else that might give us a clue. We needed insight into whether they'd brought her here, or if we should be looking somewhere else.

We fanned out, a loose chain of sorts, picking our way through an uneven field off a county road west of Fort Worth, prodding at the shin-high buffalo grass and craggy mesquites with thin walking poles. The others' faces mirrored my own grim one, alert eyes sweeping back and forth, like a pendulum keeps time on one of those old grandfather clocks. In our case, time was the enemy. The longer we searched, the more likely a dark outcome. My heart squeezed at the thought, a sourness flooding my mouth. *God. She might be dead. Please, please, please, don't be dead.*

Shrieks of a whistle broke the silence, and our chain abruptly stopped for a water break, each of us drifting slightly apart. I plucked at the grimy t-shirt glued to me, longing for air to circulate. Anything to cool down. Not only was it Hades-like in this field, but my thoughts were like open flames licking at the inside of my brain. Why had she kept secrets from me, lied to me? What was I missing, and more importantly, who could I trust? Everything in my world was burning down.

"How you doin', Hun?" the woman beside me asked. Earlier, she'd told me her name was Dee, as we'd congregated around the back of a pickup truck, sharing doughnuts and coffee in the muted light of dawn. She was tall, about my height, but with a slighter frame. I watched as she upended a bottle of water, a series of loud gulps following, until she downed every ounce, a satisfied slurp at the end. She looked as miserable as I felt. Her jeans were dirt-stained, and her button-down shirt was soaked through at the armpits. Glancing at her leather hiking boots, and then at my now torn-up canvas sneakers, it was clear Dee had done this before. She cocked her head, thick brows hovering above the aviators.

"You drinkin' enough?"

I stared at the brushy path ahead and nodded, lying, of course, my throat still stinging. The late morning sun blazed above. I checked the cloudless sky for birds, those huge black carrion-eaters, the ones my mom believed were summoned by Death. They'd appear out of nowhere, circling and bobbing on invisible strings, pushed upward on thermals that shimmered from the sweltering Texas soil. Those scavengers would scan the ground just as thoroughly as we were, looking for signs of anything weak enough they could swoop down and pick apart. But, for now, no birds were in sight.

Overhead was a canvas of baby blue, beautiful in its starkness. Not that I appreciated the endless field and sky in front of me. The total isolation creeped me out. Three unopened bottles of water swished behind me in my backpack but reaching for one required too much effort. I didn't want to waste the time. We were running out of it. Fear expanded in my belly, threatening to overcome what little hope I was clinging to. Each passing minute might determine whether we found her alive. Or dead. But I couldn't comprehend that last part, really. Couldn't go there at all.

A rancher had called in this tip last night after watching the local news. He'd noticed a car, fitting a similar description as the one given to the public, wandering the back roads near his property late yesterday afternoon. A group of volunteers immediately set up this morning's search. But what if it wasn't the same car? What if we were way off, hundreds of miles, maybe, from where she was? The thought pressed against my heart, my mind spinning on and on with "What ifs." I crunched grit between my teeth, the tang of bug spray mixed with salty soil coming to life. But I didn't care. I'd eat the damn dirt and drink gallons of bug spray if it meant bringing her home safe.

Almost forty-eight hours she'd been missing. I eyed the volunteers around me, most speaking quietly, as if we were at Mass. A part of me felt like I was floating somewhere above, watching it all go down. This couldn't be real. It had to be a nightmare, a horrible dream from which I'd soon wake. Had to be. I mean, why had they taken her? Had she known them, or was it a rando attack? Was she hurt? Was she calling, waiting for help to arrive? I scanned the miles before me. Our group was puny compared to the vastness that surrounded us. The search group's drone operators were working another missing person case and wouldn't be here for hours, if at all today. My insides itched to keep moving, knowing we needed to hurry. I wanted to scream: *Let's go! No time for fucking water breaks, people!*

A biting fly buzzed near my cheek. I swatted at it, cursing. The feeling of helplessness was stifling, almost as much as the 99-degree temperature. I couldn't take much more. She could be hidden anywhere out here. I looked at my watch. Four minutes had gone while we stood around. Couldn't these people walk and drink at the same time?

"If it's not the damn flies, it's those heartless fire ants," Dee muttered, slapping at her shins before straightening. "Bunch o' dumbasses."

She ran a hand under the gray-streaked braid at her nape, unwrapping the handkerchief at her throat, drenching it with water. "Lord o'mercy," she said as she re-knotted it, "it's baking out here. Gotta stay hydrated, Hun. Sure you're drinkin' enough water?"

I ignored her. *Stop talking.* I shot her a look before returning my gaze to the sky. But she was one of those who didn't read social cues. *Socially obtuse.* That's how my best friend Cici would describe her—with her signature eyeroll, of course.

"It's looking pretty bad out here, huh?" She tried again. "This place—it's just too big to cover on our own, ya know?" She sighed. "We sure could use some more folks out here, but whatever. It'd take divine intervention to locate anyone in these parts. Poor woman. Sure would be easy for whoever took her to make sure she'd never be found—know what I mean?"

I could have strangled her for saying that. When I didn't answer, Dee nodded her chin my way. "So, what do you think?"

That you need to shut the fuck up. Again, I looked at my watch. Six minutes. The space between my eyes throbbed in time with my heartbeat. I chewed my lip, silently counting to fifty before responding. Get a grip, Mireya. She's a volunteer trying to help someone she doesn't even know. Plus, she doesn't know who I am, I reminded myself. It's not her fault she's socially obtuse. Cici might say I was the major dumbass here. She also might say I was projecting my frustration and anger on this poor woman.

"We'll find her," I managed through chapped lips. "Maybe not here, but—we have to stay positive." I forced myself to grab a water from my pack, taking a long swallow, even though my stomach protested. I shrugged the pack on and reached for my walking poles just as the whistle sounded. The break was over. We were on the move again.

About ten minutes later, I heard it—the whiny hum of an engine—followed by plumes of dust trailing in the air as it bounced along about 200 yards in front. A four-wheeler raced toward us. The all-terrain vehicles had passed our group much earlier on reconnaissance duty. The driver, a leather-faced man with a tuft of gray hair, motioned for us to stop. His expression remained guarded as he rolled to a halt near the leader of our group, pulling off dust-coated sunglasses.

His voice was quiet, his speech drawn out. We all stopped, straining to catch bits of words carried by the gentlest hint of wind— "Looks like... don't know, but maybe...shallow grave...."

Two large birds suddenly appeared in the sky. They glided in circles above, about a half mile from where we stood. Their presence told me all I needed to know.

I bit back nausea and dropped the poles to the ground, hunching over with hands on knees. *Stay strong, Mireya,* I heard my mother whisper, above the noisy thudding of my heart, a soothing voice, as light as the faint breeze caressing my sweaty cheeks. *Stay strong.* I looked up and steadied my gaze on the leader of our search party.

He was an older guy named Gary, with bird legs and a small pot belly. When he spoke, which was seldom, he never seemed to look anyone directly in the eyes. Turns out he'd lost his child to a predator years ago. The monster who had confessed was on death row in Huntsville for killing six other young boys, but the body of Gary's son—a round-faced kid with sandy bangs above smiling blue eyes—had never been found. The predator couldn't remember where he'd dumped it, or even when it had happened, but he'd kept the kid's Hot Wheels as a trophy.

Gary lumbered in my direction, downcast, rolling a long blade of grass between his fingers, stopping in front of me. The weight of his sigh sounded in the hushed silence, as everyone on the chain openly stared. I'm sure they wondered why he had walked over to me. He was the only one who knew why I was here and what this search meant to me. I focused on the tips of his work boots, covered in dirt and grass stains, the same that marked the frayed bottom of his Wranglers. He squatted down to look me in the face, let loose the blade of grass, which fluttered to the ground at my feet.

"Hey." He appeared out of focus, haloed by a darkness that pushed at his face. "Listen—you okay?"

A dumb question considering where we were, what we were doing. I blinked twice. Suddenly, I couldn't pull in enough oxygen, couldn't find my voice.

"Sure," I managed to croak. My head bobbed up and down, my vision blurred, the blackness closing in around the outline of his face.

He reached out, placing a hand on my forearm. I flinched from the touch, what it might mean. He cleared his throat. The flies. I could hear them all around us. *Buzzing, buzzing.* Louder and louder.

"I need you to stay put. They, uh, found something not too far from here." So, this was really happening. The world in front of me began rocking. He gripped my arm tighter. "But let's be clear, okay? We're not certain who it is—it looks to be a woman, but we can't be sure—we don't know if it's your mom."

Your mom. Those were the last words I made out. I squinted hard at the eyes in front of me, two splotches the color of pool water, saw his mouth moving, everything slowing down, time stumbling, falling. I felt myself slip under, saw his face above me blur into lighter blues, then fade of all color into nothing.

Mija, please. Stay strong. Again, I heard the whisper, fierce this time, but I had lost the source of it. I had let her go. Sinking into the cool depths of the void, I was enveloped by the whispery shadows of carrions circling overhead.

Chapter 2

Three Days Missing

I woke up sprawled on the grass, with volunteers crowded around me. I'd been out maybe a minute, if that. I struggled to my feet, my rubbery limbs not wanting to cooperate.

"I've got this," I mumbled, using my walking poles to pull myself into a standing position, more diagonal leaning than upright. I wobbled, clutching the poles like two thin lifelines.

I heard the somber chatter from Gary's hand-held two-way radio—something about a finger discovered near a mound of clawed soil. Something about a tallish, blonde, naked woman, found in a shallow grave not far from where we stood. The imagery too horrific for me to fully digest.

Thank God, it wasn't her. Mom was just over five-feet, her hair the color of coal. I was simultaneously relieved and sickened, as I fully grasped that even though it wasn't her, it was someone else's mother or sister or daughter left in the middle of nowhere, carelessly dumped in a grave so insubstantial that wild animals had already snatched a few of the bones.

This world *was* a fucking jungle. Plain and simple. It wasn't just something Mom constantly harped on, how danger existed at every turn. And she was alone in it, facing predators on her own. I let go of the poles, watched them splay out in front, then hunched over and vomited the water I had sucked down earlier, as my fellow searchers tried to steady me at arm's length.

"For the love—give her some breathing room," Gary yelled, causing the others to back away even more. He clicked off the radio. "Mireya? Hey. It's gonna be okay."

That was laughable. No, I wouldn't ever be okay, but whatever. Someone moved beside me, lightly patting my back. I stiffened, not wanting anyone near me, except for my mom. But she wasn't there, was she? I was scared, but pissed, too. She'd peddled a shitload of lies, made me believe we had a decent life together, and then—poof—she was gone in seconds with no explanations. Who was she, anyway? Was she the woman I looked up to or was she that person the police suspected might be involved in criminal activity? I believed she was the former, but who was I kidding? I didn't know squat. Why hadn't she trusted me enough to tell the truth?

"It's gonna be alright, Hun," that lady Dee murmured next to me. Would it? Really? I called bullshit on that. She had no idea of the black hole—the vacuum caused by Mom's abduction and disappearance—swirling in the middle of my universe, fueled by more questions than answers about my mom, sucking up the reality of our life as I knew it. I tried to form words but couldn't make my mouth move properly. I heard Dee say to Gary in a muffled voice, "I knew she wasn't drinking enough. She's dehydrated."

My teeth chattered as I dropped to my knees again on the rocky soil. It hurt, but I didn't care. I stared at the barf in front of me, my body dry-heaving, but pulling up nothing from an empty stomach.

"Get her back to base! Earl will take care of her," a man yelled, or maybe it was Gary.

Within seconds, I was lifted to the four-wheeler where they encircled my arms around the driver's waist. He smelled of stale sweat, and my nose scrunched in protest, my stomach gurgled another warning.

I wanted to object, but my limbs felt as limp as a torn balloon. We bounced along the pasture, up and over thickets of buffalo grass, my teeth clacking against each other. I leaned the side of my forehead against him and stared out into the expanse of nowhere, my eyelids fighting to stay open. *How will I find you? What have they done to you?* I asked, just before I slipped into a yellow-red world of unconsciousness.

***

I dreamed she was laughing, a joyful sound erupting from deep within her belly. We sat at the kitchen table, the aroma of green chili chicken en-chiladas, her signature dish, surrounding us, causing my mouth to water. Her hair was streaked with thin tendrils of silver sprouting randomly at the crown of her head, like she hadn't been to the hairstylist in a while.

I stared at her, soaking in every inch of her beauty.

"What are you looking at, mija? Has it hit you what an old woman I've become?" she asked playfully. Her warm eyes had fine wrinkles at the corners, and her face was bare of makeup. She had her hair pulled into a messy bun; a soft downy widow's peak dipped on her forehead. A thought struck me. She'd only been seventeen when she'd had me. The same age I was now.

We worked a jigsaw puzzle, one of her favorite things to do. There was always a working puzzle on our table, with each of us finding pieces in spare moments or when we sat down to catch up on each other's days. This one dealt with animals, some National Geographic image, but I couldn't work out what they were supposed to be. The pieces in front of me all blurred into splotches of color. Varying grays and yellows and oranges.

"I can't find anything," I groaned, looking up at her face. Her brow furrowed. She didn't like when I whined like that, and she detested when I said the phrase "I can't" even more. I rubbed my temples, staring hard at the hazy images before me. Why was it so difficult to see the pieces?

"Look! Look right in front of you," she said, sharply. My face burned with shame. I'd never liked disappointing her. "Can't you see it? You're not looking hard enough."

I grabbed a puzzle piece and tried to force it into the blob of colors. Nothing fit. The shapes were all wrong. Nothing made sense.

"Wait. What are you talking about? I don't see it!" A panic rose inside me. A high-pitched zinging in my ears, my vision listing. "You lied! I can't see it!"

Her voice changed again. Melodic, with a hint of a smile. "Reach out, mija. You will find it—I know you will." Confused, I looked at my mother, but her features were fading. Bursts of colors first and then steadily dimming. The back of her fingers, cool to the touch, brushed my cheek.

"Look around," she said just before fading into shadows, "sometimes the answers are right in front of you."

***

"That's right." I heard a man's gravelly voice. "Reach that arm out—yeah, just like that. That a way, sweetheart."

My eyes slowly opened to the sight of lips moving under a salt-and-pepper beard. We were under a shady canopy next to a long, white pickup truck.

"Hey there, young lady. Name's Earl," the bearded man said, sliding the blood pressure cuff off my bicep. "Glad to see you come around." He dabbed a cool, damp washcloth on my forehead, then laid it across my brow. It felt like heaven. What little light there was under the canopy stabbed at my eyes, forcing me to squint at him. I was lying on a camp cot, my head propped up on a small pillow. "Can you tell me your name?" He wore a backwards baseball cap and a beat-up work shirt, the collared kind usually worn at auto shops. I smelled tobacco chew and beer in the air. Or maybe I was imagining that?

"Mireya," I mumbled.

"Well, Mireya, it's right good to meet ya," he said, reaching for a water bottle and uncapping it next to me. "So, I'm gonna give you a tiny sip, but just a tiny one, see. Don't gulp it. You drink too fast, and you'll get sick again. Got it?"

I nodded, even though I wanted to rip the bottle from him and guzzle it. A thirst I'd never fathomed had overcome me. The taste of dirt covered my tongue, as did the leftover taste of puke. I needed a gallon of water to wash it away, make me feel normal again.

He tilted the bottle toward me and dribbled a small amount into my mouth. It trickled down my throat, but not enough. Not nearly enough. Earl asked me more questions and offered more small amounts of water at intervals, until I was eventually able to sit up and drink regularly.

My brain began to sputter to life, processing the situation, the dream that I'd had. What was my mom talking about? Were there answers right in front of me? Could I figure out what she had been up to? Would that lead me to her? Could I figure it out and save her?

"So, Mireya, what brings you out here? Haven't seen you before on any of our searches." The canopy swayed as the wind whipped up, the blue tarp flapping against the gusty currents. As inconspicuously as he could, Earl spat tobacco juice into an empty Coke can, and set it down next to his lawn chair. "You a student of that missing teacher?"

"Yessir." I didn't tell him that I was her daughter. I didn't need pity to distract me right now. I needed focus.

"Right kind of you to come out here. We need all the help we can get." Earl looked skeptical, but didn't ask any more questions. He helped me sit up, then passed an orange to me. "That should make ya feel better."

"Thank you," I said, glancing at him. He looked about my uncle's age, the same type of buzz cut. "Do you do this a lot? I mean—search for people?"

"Yep," he puffed his cheeks before blowing out a sigh, "too often, I'd say."

The answers to what I was looking for were right in front of me. Like mom said in the dream. I just needed to figure out what those pieces were, how they fit together, and piece by piece, they'd lead me to her.

"Do they know who she was?" I asked, speaking to the half-eaten orange cupped in my palms.

"Who we talkin' about, sweetheart?"

"The woman," I said, gesturing in the direction where they'd discovered the grave. "The body they found. Do they know who she might be?"

Earl looked past my shoulder. "The sad thing is, it could be any one of them. Any of the thousands missing."

I shuddered. *Thousands*? In that moment an image blazed on the backs of my eyelids. The animal puzzle in the dream. I saw it clearly now—an image of a mother elephant charging, fighting to defend its calf from an angry bull. *I had to figure this out, what she had been trying to tell me in the dream.* Our roles had switched. And one fact was certain: I'd bulldoze my way through hell to protect her. I couldn't let her become one of the thousands.

CHAPTER 3

The Morning She Went Missing

Mom kissed me goodbye, holding me tighter than usual. She buried her nose in my hair, still damp from a shower. I felt her smile against me.

"Hmmm," she murmured as she inhaled. "Smells like coconuts."

I'm not sure why, but I allowed her to hold me, something I'd rarely let her do these days. Maybe it was because I'd been a jerk the night before, snapping at her when she popped her head inside my room as I was texting Cici. Sometimes my temper got the best of me, especially when she hovered. This morning, though, my body relaxed against hers, like when I was younger, letting it go when her arms brushed the slight padding above my hips, an area that made me insanely self-conscious. I felt generous as I circled my arms about her, sinking my cheek into the side of her neck, breathing in hints of baby powder. Since I could remember, she'd rub powder on the roots when she was running late and didn't have time to wash her hair—a trick her abuela had passed on. I tried to tell her that dry shampoo spray would achieve the same thing, but she thought it was ridiculous to spend ten bucks on a bottle that didn't last as long. We stood there, simply hugging, as if swaying in a gentle wind, a dance we hadn't performed in so long but remained second-nature. These arms had provided me with safety my entire life, and, yet lately I hadn't wanted what they'd offered. Instead, I longed to be in the arms of another certain someone by the name of Luka, a senior debater I was crushing on at school.

Mom sighed, then shifted in my arms.

"Maybe we can do something fun together? This weekend?" she said, her voice edged with a rasp. "We could work outside in the garden or take a drive to the lake?"

"Maybe."

"I'd like that very much," she said, wistfully, pulling back to look at me. Her palms cradled the sides of my face. "Gives me something to look forward to."

Something was up with her, I could see it in the intensity of her stare, but I didn't want to get into it. Maybe I should have. The past few weeks, I'd noticed she'd been more preoccupied than usual, focused on prepping her eighth-grade math students for another standardized test. The teachers freaked out about it. So much emphasis was put on their students' test performances. My mom's classes always scored well above the statewide average, but she set the bar high, even for those who weren't in advanced classes. Almost obsessive about it, she wanted her kids to be 100 percent prepared for what they'd face on the test. But this year she seemed even more intense, if that was possible.

Her usual easy smile had been slower to surface, and creases furrowed her brow. Without her glasses, my mom's usual lively eyes, a sparkling amber, were slightly bloodshot. It was obvious she hadn't been sleeping much. But, despite her exhausted appearance, her body language conveyed a different story. She had been on high alert, edgy. If the crepe myrtle branches so much as scraped against our front window, or a car door slammed a few doors down, she'd abruptly freeze and frown into the distance. After evaluating the sound, she'd fan her face, and resume whatever it was she'd been doing.

"You stressed out? Anything else going on besides test prep?" I asked, halfheartedly, aware that the morning was slipping away. "You were still up last night when I turned out the light. That was, like, what—one in the morning?"

"Who's the mother here?" she teased. "You know how it gets this time of year. I'll be better when it's all over."

It made sense. The spring semester was always hectic for her. Part of me knew she was hiding more, but, if I'm honest, I didn't want a lengthy explanation of what was making her worn-out and skittish. I was distracted myself, focusing on literature homework; preparing my case for a debate tournament in two weeks; and, of course, daydreaming about Luka, tall and lanky, who was the most talented speaker on our team. And his smile? Pure fire. That, along with the demands of high school life kept me from fully focusing when I was with her. It didn't help I'd lied to her last night about my plans today, or that I'd been hiding another secret from her—that I'd sent in an ancestry DNA the day before, in hopes of learning something, anything, about my deceased father's background. I don't know why I kept it to myself, other than my instinct told me she'd be bothered by it.

Maybe it was the guilt that compelled me to release her abruptly, step away, watching impatiently as she gathered her purse and a canvas tote overflowing with books and papers, while balancing stacks of file folders in her arms. I held the door open for her—*should I help her carry things, or will that be another five minutes I can't get back?*— and watched her fumble with the key fob at the car.

Once behind the wheel, she waved while starting the engine. *Should I call to her, tell her I love her, the way I used to when I when I was younger?*

She'd like that. Would it make up for my lies? No, it wouldn't make a difference. I waved back with a flick of my wrist, then hastily closed the door, started a playlist and scrolled through social media posts while I headed to my room to get dressed for school. I hummed to music as I painstakingly put eyeliner and smoothed my hair with a flatiron, so it draped in a curtain down my back. I wanted to look my hottest for after school. I had other plans than what I'd mentioned to Mom. It was no big deal, really. It wasn't like I planned to shoot up heroin in a back alley somewhere, but Mom wouldn't have agreed to them. She would have said no if I'd asked to go with friends to watch the new Marvel movie on a school night. Cici and I had already schemed a way that I'd wind up sitting next to Luka. Maybe I'd share popcorn with him, maybe rest my arm against his at the theater. So, instead of asking, I'd lied, told Mom I'd be with the debate team, working on our cases at the public library until late. Half of it was true. Most of the team was going tonight.

Hours later, a nervous vice principal called me out of AP Calculus class, and with few words, ushered me into the principal's office where two police detectives waited—one with a wispy mustache; the other, with irises so inky black I could barely make out her pupils. My brain refused to compute most of what they said, as I huddled in a chair, dazed by their words, thick tears clouding my vision.

Mom was missing. She'd been violently abducted at an ATM about an hour after she'd left our home this morning. Apparently, she had plans she hadn't shared, either. Even though I had watched her gather her papers and stuff, seen her drive away, she had never intended to go to school. She had called in sick earlier, feigning a migraine, which was why she wasn't immediately reported missing until a bank security guard watched surveillance footage and identified her later in the morning. All of it was so out-of-character for her, so unlikely, I couldn't grasp any possible reasons for her actions. What had she been up to? Why had she lied? Maybe I could have changed the course, if I'd known what was going on. Maybe she'd be waiting for me at home, instead of gone, one of the countless faces that went missing every year.

But, really, how could anyone predict any of this? Things like this only happened in films. Not in real life. And certainly not in the uneventful lives of my mom and me. There was absolutely nothing exciting to see with us. Fact is, most people would be beyond-bored by how nerdy we were. That's what I'd always thought, anyway. Until today.

CHAPTER 4

One Day Missing

"So, was she acting differently to you? Anything out of the ordinary?" asked the detective named Anderson. He kept his voice level, a matter-of-fact tone, like whatever my response was didn't matter. I'd watched enough cop shows on television to know it did. "How did she appear this morning?"

"Tired," I said. The air around him smelled faintly like cigarettes and coffee breath. I breathed through my mouth to keep the funk at a minimum. "She was up late last night. She seemed jumpy, but I didn't think too much of it. Testing's next week. She's always stressed, even more than usual, this time of year."

I rubbed a fingertip over the soda can in front of me, swirling the condensation on the outside of it. I took a sip, but the clear fizz had no taste. The few nibbles of the cookie in front of me were as flavorful as Styrofoam. My senses had muted the instant they showed me what an ATM surveillance camera had caught on video earlier that morning. Nothing would taste, look, feel, smell or sound the same until they brought her back to me. I needed her to be okay.

"Has she ever mentioned anyone who might want to hurt her?" Detective Anderson asked. "A lover? Disgruntled students—parents—coworkers?"

I blinked, stuffed up from too much crying. I could barely breathe properly. I leveled my most withering gaze at him.

"My mother didn't have...*a lover*. And students and other teachers worship her." I blew harsh bursts into a napkin and mopped around my nose. The wadded tissue was wet and ragged, falling apart in my hands, like everything else in my life. "Everybody loves her. Ask anybody."

"Sure." He looked away, his thumb brushing the edge of his lame mustache.

I was accustomed to people looking away when I zeroed in on them. The girl with kaleidoscope eyes, that's what they sometimes called me. I had partial heterochromia in both eyes, making my irises two-toned. Lots of people had it, and it was no big deal, but mine stood out. A blue-gray made up the outer ring of my irises, with a jagged starburst of amber gold surrounding my pupils. The starburst in my right eye was larger, and the effect dizzied people. Or so I'd been told, anyway. Even my own mom sometimes averted her gaze from mine.

"Any idea why your mother was withdrawing cash from ATMs all over town yesterday?" the dark-haired cop named Cho asked me, leaning forward. The question—and what it implied—shook me. Anger surged in my veins. It was becoming obvious. These officers didn't know what the hell they were doing. And they certainly didn't know anything about my mom.

I straightened, my upper lip lifting into a sneer. "What are you talking about? We don't have a lot of cash. She's a single mom. *A teacher.* It's not like we're rolling in dough—she has a checking account and my college savings—that's it."

Both detectives were silent. Cho cocked her head and stared. She didn't believe me. *What the hell?* I shifted in my chair and returned her gaze, unblinking. *Two can play at this game, lady.*

In the end, Detective Cho won the staring contest. My impatience and disgust couldn't be contained.

"Wow. Are you fucking kidding me? What are we doing here?" I slammed both fists down on the table. "I need to find her. *You* need to be looking for her. This is bullshit—we're wasting time."

Shuffling through the file, Detective Anderson pulled out two pieces of paper and slid them toward me. My stomach plunged; my heart quickening. Both papers had account information, with Mom's name clearly printed on them. Accounts I hadn't known we had. I looked the large numbers over. I couldn't make sense of what I was seeing. Six-digits? These accounts belonged to someone else. We didn't have money like this. Never had.

"It looks like she had been withdrawing from *multiple* bank accounts, including your savings account, for the past two weeks, taking cash in small amounts at different ATMs all over town," he said. The room was silent again. My mouth-breathing sounded more ragged. "Any idea where your *teacher* mom got this kind of money, kid? Looks like she's had large sums deposited over the past year, way more than just her paychecks, from untraceable bank accounts in the Cayman Islands. Then, little by little, she has been withdrawing cash."

"What was she up to? Was she in trouble? If we had some idea what or who she was involved with, it might help us find her." He angled closer. "Time isn't on our side, Miss Torres. We don't think this was random. You saw the video, you saw those goons, right? They mean business." His voice rose. The sound ricocheted inside my brain, getting harsher. "Look, you're almost an adult, so I'm not going to coddle you. Your mother is in danger—some seriously deep shit. We need information, or we can't help her."

This was so fucked. I shook my head. No way was I hearing any of this correctly. My mom wouldn't be emptying bank accounts, especially my college savings, without telling me. We'd been saving for school since I was a toddler. Any spare change went into a large jelly jar on her bedroom dresser, which we'd take to the bank every couple of months to deposit for my education; she'd been almost obsessive about it since I was in elementary school. I had no clue where that other money had come from.

"You need to check your facts." I stared at the columns the detective had highlighted. Mom had three additional accounts I wasn't aware of, all of them adding up to more than $800,000. I tossed the paper on the table. "This isn't possible. There's no way." *Eight-hundred-thousand dollars?*

"Have you called my uncle? Angel Torres? He should be here," I said, swiping at another round of tears spilling down my cheeks. "He's in law enforcement, you know. Works for the DEA? He'll help me find her. I've called him but I haven't heard—" I'd left countless messages on his voicemail and texted him close to fifty times. But he hadn't responded, yet.

"Yes, we finally got ahold of him. He's on his way back." Detective Anderson said, drumming his fingers against his biceps. "We located him in Maui with his girlfriend. His flight gets in this afternoon."

"Okay." I swallowed hard. *His girlfriend? What girlfriend? What the hell? Had I stepped into an alternate reality?*

The jerk slid another piece of paper toward me. Highlighted were a series of withdrawals made minutes apart at different ATMs across the city. The last one had been made this morning at the ATM in a bougie town-square area about twenty minutes from our house. The same ATM where she was abducted just seconds after slipping cash into her purse. The ATM camera also showed the sudden blinding fear in her face that screamed, "*Help me!*" Two men wearing ski-masks had come from behind, one pressing a gun to her temple before yanking her out of the camera's view. Another nearby surveillance camera had captured them pushing her into the back seat of her small sedan, caught the interrupted scream as one of them slammed her head against the roof. She fought, then crumpled. The blur of another man jumping behind the wheel, throwing the car into reverse, and speeding out of the parking lot.

"I don't understand." The paper began shaking in my hand, and the numbers blurred. I wiped away the tears with annoyance.

Where had all the money come from? What had my mom been up to? She was just a teacher. A math and science nerd who bought most of her clothes from thrift stores and clipped coupons for groceries. Just a mom. My mom. These accounts had to be wrong. And who the hell were those guys covered from head-to-toe in black? It had to be random. She just happened to be at the wrong place this morning. Yes. That was it. But why did they abduct her and not just take her money and car? My gut told me something else was happening here, though I didn't know what it could be. It also told me I had to do everything I could to find her, figure this nightmare out fast. She had always been the strong one in our family, the one who took care of everyone. But she needed me to be that now. I had to find a way to help her—to get her away from those scumbags and back home where she belonged.

I pressed the heels of my hands against my skull, that image of her terrified face still visible before me. No matter how hard I pushed, the image stayed. *Mami,* I cried inside my head, *please hold on. I'm coming for you.*

CHAPTER 5

Two Days Missing

P olice suspect foul play. The phrase tumbled through my brain on a loop. Things around me whirled in slow motion each time I turned my head. I stared blankly at the television on the wall in a small waiting room at the police station. The local evening news led with my mother's abduction, a story picked up by news agencies across the country a few hours earlier.

After airing the clip of the ATM security video, the plastic-haired anchor cleared his throat with the gravity of an undertaker.

"Police are seeking information from anyone who might have seen eighth-grade teacher Ana María Torres or either of the suspects seen in this image," he said. "Law enforcement have asked anyone with details on Ms. Torres' whereabouts to call this number immediately. They're looking for information on the two assailants, as well, but have asked citizens not to approach them if spotted. These men are considered extremely dangerous. Again, do not approach them. Call this number or 911 immediately if you see them."

Ping.... Ping.... I flinched as my phone blew up with more texts from friends. My mom was on news feeds all over social media. God, she'd hate seeing that. It took years to convince her to get a cell phone, but she'd finally compromised with a flip-phone. No smartphone for her. Besides being insanely private, she believed social media was the beginning of the end for humanity. Countless times she'd lectured me about video chat apps and texting on my phone.

"Put it away, mija. Look at *me*, not at the dummy screen," she'd say, adding, "Someday people will forget how to talk to each other. We're regressing to caveman grunts and gestures or whatever you'd compare to those ridiculous emojis. Eye contact, please." I tried to tell her nobody used emojis anymore, but she shrugged it off with a laugh and changed the subject. Now I'd give anything for just that. To bicker with her, to hear one of her never-ending lectures about the evils of social media.

Ping.... Ping.... I reached inside the back pocket of my jeans, muting the phone. Since the story had broken, a steady stream of messages flowed in from school friends, her teacher friends, her ladies' church group. People wanted to bring food. Like I could eat a tuna casserole right now. They wanted to plan volunteer searches. Make fliers. Over and over, they asked what they could do to help. As if I had a clue. Like I had a grasp on what to do when your mother disappears under violent circumstances. My mom would know what to do, but she wasn't here. I knew they meant well, but I couldn't cope with it. My brain was working at full capacity, with no room to spare. I could barely keep my shit together.

Since I'd learned of her abduction, I'd only responded to two texts. The first was our next-door neighbor, Shilpa, my mom's best friend. She was frantic, like in a total panic, so I tried my best to calm her down. The other was from Cici, my best friend and debate partner. They'd led her into the principal's office after they told me, her face pale. I'd cried in her arms most of the afternoon and last night. Her mom had picked us up, and taken me to their house, while we tried to locate my uncle.

Cici had already texted twice this afternoon since reluctantly dropping me off at the police station.

"I don't like leaving you alone. Call if you need a ride back to my house," she'd told me as I dragged myself out of her car. "Or if you need *anything*. I'm like your personal Uber driver. Got me?" She had raised those perfectly arched eyebrows of hers before slipping sunglasses back on. Then she frowned. "This is so messed up, right? But the police will find her, Mireya. We gotta have faith they're gonna find her."

I gulped in response, tears leaking out for the umpteenth time. "Yeah. I know," I croaked, with the sensation of swallowing gravel. "I'm trying."

She'd wanted to stay with me, but the police detective I'd spoken to had said my uncle was on his way from wherever the hell he'd been, so I told her to go on. I'd missed a call from Uncle Angel earlier, followed by a quick text: *Be there soon.* That's all he could come up with when his sister had been taken with a gun to her head? *Be there soon?* When I tried to call him back, it immediately went to voicemail. I figured he was working a case and couldn't risk blowing his cover. That happened in his line of work. But it pissed me off just the same.

Police suspect foul play. I buried my face in my hands. Unreal. Forty-eight hours ago, I would have thought it stupid to use that term in connection with my mom. But now? I didn't know what to think about anything. I was desperate to talk with my uncle, get his take on this madness. He'd finally shown up about a half hour ago, I was told, but had been whisked away. The police didn't even give me a chance to see or speak to him. Instead, they'd been questioning him since he arrived.

But I could see him now, as I stared through the waiting room window. He stood with two detectives in the hallway. Uncle Angel was average height with a wiry build. He had his signature pair of aviator sunglasses clipped to the neckline of a snug polo shirt, which showed off a lean, muscular torso. He looked like a young Al Pacino, my mom always said. The two of them didn't look much like brother and sister—mom's face was heart-shaped; his was gaunt with high cheekbones jutting out. But then I didn't look much like my mom, either. I had lighter skin and hair color, and a face with longer features. I must have taken after my biological father, a man who'd I'd never met because he'd died when I was a baby. I didn't even have a photo of him because all the photo albums had been lost in one of our many moves.

I tried to catch my uncle's attention, but he didn't appear to see me—he was zeroed in on the detectives, his hands on his hips, a professional cop-face in place. He listened, bowing his head every so often, his eyebrows meeting over the bridge of his nose. Whenever things were serious, he'd get that look. When I was little, he had worked Border Patrol, but he'd switched to the DEA about fifteen years ago. He had said he needed new scenery, but busting gun-toting slime balls who ran meth labs from filthy travel trailers in the middle of Podunkville, Texas, didn't sound like much of a scenic view to me. Mom and I had always worried he'd get shot in the crossfire of a drug-bust-gone-bad. We'd have never guessed it'd be my mom targeted by violence, instead.

A uniformed police officer, an older guy with white hair, leaned inside the doorway. "Miss, you need anything? Shouldn't be too much longer."

I motioned to the soda and barely touched cookies. "I'm good, thanks." He quickly darted away. A different officer had checked on me every ten minutes, it seemed, each one saying the exact thing.

I kneaded my knuckles into my forehead, trying to clear my head. What had I missed? Mom had been acting about the same as usual. Maybe she'd been a little more paranoid lately, pulling the curtains tight when she'd normally let in the afternoon sun. Circling the block because she thought a car was following too closely, and she didn't want the driver to know where we lived. She'd seen something on the news about thieves targeting people outside their garages, she'd told me. She'd refused to let me drive alone to nighttime study groups or trips to the movies, insisting she needed the car for other things and that she would drop me off and pick me up.

But my mom had always been more cautious than most. She was the one who'd call the neighbors if a stranger took too long walking his dogs around the cul-de-sac. I'd never asked, but my feeling was she'd gone through something horrible, like maybe she'd been molested as a kid growing up in New Mexico. Or maybe saw violence? (I'd asked her about it once, but she denied anything like that ever happening to her. Yet, at least once a month, she'd awaken from nightmares, shouting or screaming.) Plus, she hovered nearby all the time, constantly keeping tabs on where I went and with whom. I wasn't allowed to sleep over at friends' houses. They were welcome to sleep at our house anytime, but she wanted me with her, which was embarrassing to explain to my friends, especially as I grew older. Luckily, Cici had taken it in stride.

My mom trusted no one.

When I was five, she had insisted I enroll in martial arts, so I could learn how to defend myself. At first, I was excited, but the older I got, it became less appealing.

"Mireya, you must know how to take care of yourself. The world—it's not always a safe place—and you must learn to protect yourself," she'd told me.

At the time, I was nine and grumbling about taking taekwondo classes. The cool girls at school practiced hip-hop moves during recess, and others showed off their soccer foot dribbles. No one seemed interested in my roundhouse kicks or knife-hand strikes. They thought it was dumb for a girl. The boys in my taekwondo class made fun of me, too, until I shamed them with strategically planted kicks to the shins during sparring sessions. I'd get in trouble by the instructor for the contact, but it was well worth standing ten minutes in a corner.

"Do you think you could defend yourself with a dance move? No. If someone ever comes at you," Mom had punched her fist into the palm of her hand, "you must know how to get away. It's harsh out there—especially for girls."

I'd always bristled at that—that I was somehow more vulnerable because I was born female. It was unfair. Why would she think that way? Plus, my mom was the strongest person I knew, and she'd once been a girl.

In fact, any strength I had was on account of her. She made sure I was strong and capable. Just like her. But then again, look what had happened to her. All the measures she had taken, all the precautions, hadn't saved her from those armed thugs at the ATM yesterday.

What was taking my uncle so long? He'd been talking to the detectives for at least forty-five minutes already. He hadn't even bothered to check on me first. I forced myself to look at the television. A teacher I knew, one of my mom's friends, was being interviewed on the news. Ms. Burkett's disheveled curls stuck out about her face. She shoved a balled-up tissue in front of her nose, as she choked out words.

"I can't believe this happened. Not to Ana María," she said, her voice was wispy, barely understandable. She attempted to gather herself, her voice stronger as she looked directly into the camera. "She's an amazing person. Truly. The students and teachers just adore her. So helpful to everyone. When my mother died of cancer last year, she—" her voice broke "—she helped—my family—with the arrangements. She organized a food drop-off—"

The reporter, standing in front of the school where my mom taught, put her arm around Ms. Burkett. Students were in the background, consoling each other. Counselors were on campus to help Mom's students and coworkers cope as they heard the news, the reporter said. Some of the middle-schoolers held armfuls of printed fliers with a tip-line number and a photo from last year's yearbook, my mom's face blown up to a five-by-seven, smiling wide. She hated that photo.

This should not have happened to her. My jaws ached from clenching my teeth. An anger bubbled inside. I suddenly stood up, the chair scraping against the tile. The waiting was eating at me. I couldn't stand sitting here while she was out there, God-knows-where, possibly hurt, possibly worse. What was taking so long with Uncle Angel and those officers? I was trapped in here instead of being out there looking for her.

Without much more thought, I grabbed the soda and threw it as hard as I could at the nearby trash can. It smashed against the side and clear liquid splattered in a fan-pattern on the floor. All this crap about checking accounts or whatever. She'd be able to explain where she got that money. Truth is, I didn't really give a damn how she'd gotten it, as long as she was safe right now. She was all I cared about. We needed to find her, instead of sitting on our asses.

I lifted my chin and bellowed in frustration, "FUUUUUCK!"

My mom would hate that I used that word, especially in a public place. She'd get furious when students yelled it in the hallways. But sometimes it best summed up the state of things. I hoped she would forgive me, wherever she was.

"What the hell, Mireya?" Uncle Angel came flying through the door.

I stopped mid-wail and looked at him, my face bawling up for an ugly cry. He reached for my shoulder to steady me.

"Where were you? What's taking so long? They took her. Did you see that video? She looked so scared. Oh my God. They may hurt her. She needs us." I strung the words together quickly just before a jagged edge of despair tore at my insides, at a spot buried deep under my ribs.

I was coming undone. I'd tried to hold it together for the past twenty-four hours, but no more. The ball of panic, frustration, desperation, and fear erupted within me and flooded my body.

Uncle Angel pulled me to him, his bristled cheek scraping against mine. I struggled to catch my breath, he squeezed so hard, holding me up, murmuring, "It's okay. It's okay. It's okay." He pulled away and held my face between his hands, his thumbs brushing away the tears.

"Shhhhh. Listen, listen. I know you're scared. So am I," he said. "But we will find her. We will. I promise." I laid my palms against his chest, the sturdiness of him grounding me a bit. He cut his eyes to the doorway where the two detectives hovered. He moved closer for another hug, then whispered in my ear, "You have to pull your shit together—*get your snap*. Understand?" He paused, lowered his voice even more. "Listen—we're being watched. Closely."

I allowed myself to lean against him, even as my mind registered that this scene was off. The dark timbre of his voice, the way his gaze had darted away from mine. Alarm bells set off inside my brain. He knew something. I was sure of it.

"It'll be alright," he said, leaning in again, his words muffled by hair. "But you *have* to trust me."

I nodded against my uncle's shoulder. "Sure," I managed to whisper back, "Sure."

But I was my mother's daughter. In that instant, as a long-ago memory resurfaced, I trusted no one, not even him. After all, people could lie. Sometimes they took what wasn't theirs. They often preyed on the vulnerable. The world was as untamed as a jungle. It was a harsh lesson my mom seemed determined I learn since I was a child. Maybe it was time I listened.

CHAPTER 6

Twelve Years Earlier

I smelled popcorn on my fingers, a snack we had shared earlier that day, after we rode the carousel ride at the mall. I covered my mouth and yawned wide, then rubbed at my eyes, which watered from the salt on my fingertips. I tugged on Mamí's pants leg.

"I'm sleepy." When she didn't respond, I pulled harder. "I wanna go."

"I know, mija, but this is the only day I have to shop this sale," she said in a soothing voice, the one she used to keep me calm. "You need pretty dresses when you start kindergarten, right? You'll look like such a big girl on your first day of school! Don't worry, sweetie, it won't take too much longer. Promise."

She kissed the top of my head and continued rifling through the clothes on the rack. The sound of the hangers scraping against metal bothered me. I covered my ears and frowned. I was excited to start school with the other big kids, but I couldn't have cared less about dresses. I planned to wear my Kung Fu Panda t-shirt on the first day. And I wanted to go. *Now.*

"I'm tired—" I dragged out my words in a whine, "I don't wanna dress. I wanna sleep." But she wasn't listening.

I looked around and spotted a space where I could curl up underneath a clothes rack, maybe two steps away from her. I nestled in under it, pulling my legs to my chest.

I'd barely closed my eyes before she grabbed my hand and pulled me up. She said in a low whisper, "C'mon, kiddo, let's go." She sounded odd, but I was too tired to think about it. I just wanted to go back to my comfortable car seat where I could nap as she drove us home. I forced my legs to move quickly as we made our way, fighting to keep my eyes open. Her hand felt rougher than I was used to, and she gripped so hard, it hurt. I scrunched my face and tried to pull it away from her grasp, grumbling, but she yanked on my arm. She was walking too fast.

Mamí must be really mad at me, but I don't wanna a new dress. I want my Kung Fu Panda shirt, I thought, as I glanced up at her face.

But it wasn't her face. The woman gripping my hand wasn't Mamí. This lady wore a dark cap over orange-looking hair and had huge sunglasses that covered most of her face. My legs continued moving, but my mind locked down. I had no idea what I was supposed to do. Where was my mom? Who was this lady yanking on my arm to hurry?

Dazed, I turned my head back to look for Mamí, but we were already halfway out of the mall. I couldn't see her anymore, and it clicked that this stranger was taking me away from her. Mamí had repeatedly warned me about "Stranger Danger." And this woman was definitely a stranger to me. I twisted away from her and screamed "Mamí!" as loud as I could, in an ear-piercing shrill that I hoped my mom could hear, wherever she was. But that's all I was able to get out.

The stranger immediately lifted me off the ground and smothered my face into her shoulder, as I struggled against her. She was surprisingly strong. My mother had always made me feel safe in her arms. This stranger did not. I wanted to bite her, but Mamí had taught me it wasn't nice to do that to others. I couldn't remember if it was okay to bite strangers, though.

"Shhhh," the strange woman cooed into my ear, her sharp fingernails pinching hard just below my armpit. I shrieked into her bosom and continued to jerk in her arms, despite the burning pain. If I could get out of her hold, I could run back to my mother. I'd be safe again.

"It's naptime for this little one," she joked to a passing couple who murmured something I couldn't make out. I kicked and twisted some more, trying to get loose from her hold, but she quickened her pace.

Once the couple passed, she growled, "If you don't stop, you freaky-eyed little shit, I'll hurt your mama real good! Hear what I'm saying? I'll sneak into your house when she's sleeping— cuz I know where y'all live—and I'll carve her from head-to-toe, like a Thanksgiving turkey. It'll be all your fault she's carved up and dead."

My entire body stiffened in her arms, straight as a fence post. I didn't understand everything she was saying, but I knew I didn't want Mamí sliced like a turkey. A soft whimpering escaped my trembling lips. I tried not to make any sound, but I couldn't control it. The woman muttered and kept clutching me, so tight I could barely breathe. I heard the *swooshing* of the sliding glass doors at the mall's entrance. Then my mom's voice, soft but deadly quiet.

"Put her down." Her voice sounded scary to me.

The next thing I felt were strong hands ripping me from the woman's arms. I knew those hands. Those were hands I trusted. But then she put me on the ground behind her. She was yelling words I'd never heard before, things I didn't understand, but I could feel the heat in her voice. I wanted to hold onto her legs, but my mom charged at the stranger, shoving her onto her back, before she repeatedly kicked her in the stomach, the ribs, the side of the face. With each strike, a sickening thud filled the air. Mamí continued stomping her, even as the woman tried to slither away.

I stood behind her, speechless, my lower lip dangling, too shocked to do anything but stare. I'd never seen her like this. Ever. It frightened me, but I couldn't turn away.

Finally, she spun back toward me, eyes wild. But the look on my face must have snapped her out of her frenzy. She quickly scooped me up, as people around us called for help, surrounding the bloodied woman on the ground. My mom didn't wait for the police. She ran with me to the parking lot, hastily buckled me into my car seat, and sped through the streets toward our house.

At first, she was quiet. I was shaking, watching her in the rearview mirror. My teeth chattered even though it felt like a hundred degrees outside.

"Why, mija? WHY?" she shouted, her eyes welling up. She reached back to caress my knee while she drove. Her hand was shaking. "Don't ever let anyone do that again, Mireya. Do you hear me? Kick them, scream—do *anything* to get away. Then run for help."

"She was going to hurt you," I whimpered, shrinking into my seat. "Cut you like a turkey."

She looked at me in the reflection of the rearview mirror and shook her head. She was disappointed in me. That hurt. Tears clouded my eyes. And she had frightened me back there with the lady. I had never seen anyone hit someone like that before, the blood everywhere, the wild look on her face. Especially not from the person I felt safest with in the whole world.

"No crying right now, Mireya. Please. It's important you listen. You must understand what I tell you." She held the steering wheel with one hand and ran the other through her sweaty hair. "Do not let anyone fool you—she wasn't going to hurt me. She lied to you, so you'd be afraid—so you would go without a fight. But I want you to always fight if someone tries that again. Always. Do you understand? It's important."

I nodded with a sniffle. She stopped at the red light and turned to look at me hunched over in my seat.

"You can't trust anyone, mija. I'm so sorry, sweetie, but it's true," she said, her voice breaking, as she reached back and gently wiped my tears with her thumb. "I don't know what I would have done if that animal had taken you."

At that moment, I felt the weight of her fear settle on my shoulders. She couldn't trust me to stay safe on my own. To not walk away with a stranger without putting up much of a struggle. If she hadn't saved me, I would have been taken by the scary monster, whoever she was. I realized then I would always need my mother's protection, even though she never said anything like that to me. She didn't need to. I could see for myself. She was tougher than I could ever be, shielding me from the ugliness in the world, something I couldn't manage on my own. I mean, kicking that woman the way she had? Beating her bloody? I hoped I never saw anything like it again.

CHAPTER 7

Two Days Missing

The silence pressed down on us, as we drove west on Main Street. Each bump on the road rattled my teeth. My head throbbed. We rode low to the ground in a sleek sports car that Uncle Angel had recently leased. That's the story he'd given me anyway, as he'd gestured toward the hot red sports car in the parking lot outside the station. It couldn't have been more opposite to the no-frills pickup trucks he'd driven for years.

"This? Really?" I said, giving him the side eye before climbing inside. "Whatever." The car screamed mid-life crisis to me. Maybe that's what was going on with him.

"You hungry?" He drummed fingers against the black leather steering wheel. "I'm starving. Wanna stop somewhere?" he asked. His voice was casual, as if the world wasn't exploding around me. Around us. We were in the middle of a shit storm, and he wanted a sandwich?

I glared at him in response. A country song on the car stereo twanged in the background—something about perfume, cheating hearts, and whiskey. The music fit, I thought, gritting my teeth to brace for another bump.

"Explain, please. What was that about at the police station?" I asked. "That thing about them watching us? Why would they watch us? They should be focusing on the men who took Mom, not us."

"Don't worry. We'll talk while we eat, Mireya. I need time to think." He slowed to a stop at a red light and watched pedestrians pass in front of us, then turned to meet my narrowed gaze. "Listen. You have to trust me."

"Trust you? Yeah, you keep saying that," I said, my voice rising. "Where the hell have you been, anyway? Hawaii? The fuck. I didn't know anything about you going to Hawaii. And since when do you have *a girlfriend*?" I squinted harder at him. "Mom has been missing—*gone for more than twenty-four hours*—and no one knows where the hell you are?"

"Look, I was on assignment, okay? Settle down," he said, tossing a scathing look at me. "The girlfriend is part of a cover. That's all I can say. You know I can't discuss the cases I'm working."

"Of course, you can't," I scoffed. "You're off, undercover, in Hawaii of all places, while Mom was kidnapped at gunpoint fifteen minutes from our house. I texted you like five hundred times, lost track of how many voicemails I left, none of which you responded to, by the way. But you can't—or won't—talk about what you've been up to? Seems convenient." The light turned green, and we flew through the intersection, as Uncle Angel laid on the gas pedal. I gripped the door handle with white knuckles, cursing him under my breath.

"Convenient? What are you saying? You don't believe me?" he finally asked, changing lanes. "You're being ridiculous. I was working in a situation where I couldn't check my cell phone. You think I'm okay with the fact that this happened to my sister, and I didn't even know about it?"

There was a beat of silence before I blurted, "Well—do you? What I mean is, do you know anything about what happened?"

"Wow." He shook his head, his eyes on the road. "I can't believe this shit. Think about who you're talking to here. You're seriously losing it, kid."

The muscles in my uncle's jaw continued working, as he eased onto the tollway, the engine growling in acceleration. He weaved in and out of traffic. Between his aggressive driving, my pounding head, and the chemical smell of new car, I wanted to hurl. God. I was so confused. Maybe I was overreacting.

We headed in the direction of our neighborhood. "Yeah, I may be losing it," I said. My eyes stung. I had just accused my uncle—someone who always had my back, praised my paintings, attended my taekwondo rank tests, listened to my debate speeches, my own flesh and blood—of maybe knowing something about my mom's disappearance. It was beyond horrible. "I'm sorry. I just don't understand what's—"

I hunched over, with tears flooding my cheeks. I didn't know what was what anymore. My mom was missing. My life had spun out of control. Uncle Angel sighed, patting my back.

"It's okay, little one. This is a lot," he said with a heavy voice, "I'm freaked out, too. But we'll figure this shit out—I promise. Hang in there, okay?"

I tried to pull myself together. It had to be true. He'd do everything he could to find her. He loved her as much as I did. The two of them shared an unspoken language, both guarded about the past, exchanging wary glances when I'd ask about their childhoods or their parents.

Loud gurgles from Uncle Angel's stomach interrupted my thoughts.

"Sorry." He patted a non-existent waist. "Like I said, I gotta eat, Mireya. You know how "hangry" I get. I only had time for a pack of peanuts and some crackers on the plane this morning."

"Okay, okay." I gave him a half-smile, wiping at my damp face.

"Thank god." He whipped into the parking lot of a cafe where mom and I always went. Our house was nearby, less than a mile away. As soon as we walked in, Shirley, one of our regular waitresses, spotted us. She dashed toward me, dragging me to her substantial bosom.

"Oh, Honey. I saw it on the TV. I just can't believe it." She crushed me to her body, pushing my face into bunched-up dreadlocks. "I told my husband, 'Holy shit, Howard, that's Ana María, one of my favorite regulars. I know her and her beautiful daughter.' Lord o' mercy, what is this world coming to?" Her voice carried. Other diners in the restaurant stared. She swiped tears from rouged cheeks, then stepped back and gave me a once-over. "Oh, no ma'am. You don't look good, sweetie. C'mon, now, lemme get your usual table. Bet you haven't had a single decent thing to eat."

I introduced my uncle, who insisted on sitting at a booth by a window, which faced the front door and overlooked the parking lot. He scanned the menu and quickly ordered a BLT with chips and water. I asked for a Cobb Salad and Diet Dr Pepper out of habit.

"That diet soda is poison," Uncle Angel said, as Shirley walked away.

"Whatever. You say that every time," I shot back. But I was too weary to manage our usual banter. I leaned on my elbows. Exhaustion had settled deep in my bones. My uncle watched the parking lot through the window. Then he turned somber eyes on me.

"So? You gonna tell me what's happening? What you know?" I asked.

"Mireya, did you tell the police everything? You have to tell me every word, every movement, your mom made yesterday. What did she say to you before she left? Her exact words. Did she seem scared—or agitated?" He reached for my hand, enfolding it between his warm palms. For some reason, the gesture was unnerving, instead of comforting. I couldn't say why, except his sober mood meant he was as afraid as I was. "Did she ask you to tell me anything?"

"What? What do you mean? That's a weird question." I pulled my hands from his and scraped fingers through my lank hair. He didn't respond, watching me with intensity. I shifted in my seat.

"No. Nothing about you. She was going to work, carrying a bunch of graded papers. She hugged me, asked if we could hangout this weekend—" I choked up at the image, then continued, "but she didn't say anything unusual. I thought she was going to work. I had no idea—" I rubbed the base of my neck. "Why would she ditch school like that? She never missed work. And why would she withdraw money, money I didn't know we had? Did you know that she had all that? And where in the hell did she get it? Like hundreds of thousands of dollars. The detectives think I'm hiding something, but I don't know where it came from or why she had it. She never mentioned a thing about it, which is weird, right? Does any of it add up to you?"

"I'm not sure what she was doing," he said, squinting out the window again. "None of it makes sense. But the police are suspicious of us."

"But, why? I just don't get this," I said, searching his eyes for any indication, but his gaze stayed blank.

"It's not unusual to check into family and friends," he said in a hushed voice. "They're trying to establish who might benefit if something were to happen to the victim. In Ana María's case, they found those bank accounts, which looks fishy for us since both our names are listed as TOD."

"TOD? What's that mean?"

"Transfer on death," he said after shifting in his seat. "It means the two of us are listed as beneficiaries on the accounts."

"Oh." What else could I say. No wonder the police thought we might be involved. This shit storm kept getting darker.

We sat quietly in the booth, each of us lost in our own thoughts.

The food arrived in record time. Shirley placed the plates and drinks in front of us. "This is on the house, Hon. It's the least we can do for your sweet mama," she said, sniffling. Emotion overtook me, so much so I could barely speak. I whispered my thanks, and she retreated to the front counter.

My uncle wolfed down his sandwich, his gaze darting between my face, the front door and the parking lot. He crunched on chips, while I picked at the sliced avocado and turkey in my salad, not tasting much, but aware I needed fuel. *Was something off with her? Something I missed? Was Uncle Angel hiding something?*

"Mireya?" He startled me. I'd almost forgotten he was sitting across from me. He lowered his voice. "I have to ask you, did your mom ever—did she ever mention a man? Someone she knew from a long time ago when she was younger? I know it might not make sense to you, but I need to know if she said anything about a man. It might help me find her."

"What do you mean? What man?" I blinked several times. My uncle stared back with dark eyes, unflinching, as if trying to send me a silent message.

"Wait. Was mom seeing someone?" I asked, my voice rising.

"Keep it down," he said, glancing around us, not answering my question. I shook my head, my brain fuzzy. I couldn't understand what he was getting at, no matter how hard I tried to follow.

"But—"

"No more. Not here," Uncle Angel said, as a movement in the parking lot caught his attention. He put on his sunglasses, his knee bouncing under the table. He and my mom were two of the jumpiest people I'd ever known.

"Hurry up, huh?" he motioned to the unfinished salad. "We can talk at the house. We need to leave."

"I'm done," I said, pushing the salad bowl away and standing up.

He moved in front of me, all protective like a bodyguard, and headed for the door. I followed a step behind and thanked Shirley one more time.

As I ducked into the car, I watched through the restaurant window as Shirley bussed our table. Such a normal action, really. I'd seen her do it hundreds of times. But that normal was gone from my life the minute Mom was attacked at that ATM. Things were getting more and more strange by the day, if that were possible, and I worried that *strange* might actually be my new *normal*.

I eyed my uncle behind the wheel as he drove toward our house. One thing was sinking in: He knew something, at least more than he was letting on. I had no clue what guy he was asking about or why, but he wouldn't ask if he didn't have a reason. My mom had never mentioned any dude. She was secretive about everything, including her dating life, if she even had one. In all my years, I had never known her to be romantically involved with anyone.

But there was someone else who might know more than me. If my mom confided in anyone, it'd be Shilpa. It wasn't unusual for those two to be chatting non-stop, then clam up when I'd entered the room.

"When we get home, pack a bag to take to my house. Whatever clothes and things you need. You'll be staying with me for a while. Try to make it quick, though. I have a shit-ton of calls to make," Uncle Angel said, as he turned into our neighborhood.

"Mireya?" he asked when I didn't respond. "Did you hear me? I need you to focus, okay? It's like you're on another planet."

"Huh? Yeah. Sure. I'll grab clothes and stuff for school," I said, impatiently. "But, first, there's someone I need to talk to."

As soon as he pulled into our driveway, I hopped out of the car. Maybe she was the one who could shine light on what Mom had been up to. Maybe she was one of the missing pieces I was after.

CHAPTER 8

Two Days Missing

"Oh, my god. It's you!" I heard her muffled shout from behind the door. Loud clicks followed, as she unlatched deadbolts and flung the front door wide. Her ebony eyes searched my face before embracing me.

"My darling! Are you okay?" She inched back and peered at my uncle who stood behind me.

"Hi, Shilpa," I whispered, gulping back emotion. Her shoulders seemed birdlike under a baggy Oxford shirt, so I loosened my hold on her, afraid I would hurt her.

My eyes stung at the touch of her—her hugs felt so much like Mom's. I didn't want to let her go. Shilpa Reddy had been my mom's closest friend for years. I remembered how when we first moved into our house, she'd brought over cookies, which she'd unknowingly burned. The two had erupted into giggles as Mom tried to bite one, almost breaking a tooth. They'd been inseparable for the past five years we lived here, the longest we'd ever stayed in one place.

"Hey." Uncle Angel sounded stiff. I could never figure out why he acted this way with Shilpa, but it was mutual. They just didn't jive. But my uncle could be like that with certain people. Distant and dismissive. Maybe it was the cop in him.

Shilpa gave him an abrupt nod. "Any news on Ana María?" She fingered reading glasses hanging on a cord around her neck. Her hair was pulled into a severe bun, emphasizing thick eyebrows and bloodshot eyes. Her clothes looked rumpled, like she'd been in them a while. My guess was she hadn't slept much last night. She was older than Mom, but you'd never guess she was in her late fifties. She'd pass for early forties easy.

"No news, but they're working on it," Uncle Angel said, hands shoved in the front pockets of his jeans.

Without thinking, I moved to step inside, but Shilpa blocked me with her body and the door, ducking onto the porch. To make room, I sidestepped a pot of withered flowers. Since her son had taken a job in D.C. last year, she struggled to maintain the two-story house on her own. She hired lawn workers, but no one was allowed past the entryway. Unless it was an emergency, like the time the water heater broke and flooded two bedrooms. I could still see the paleness of her face, the grave violation in her eyes, as workers tramped back and forth into her home.

Mom was the exception, though. She'd often pop over for visits or to help with minor repairs. My mom would tell me about their lengthy discussions on the universe or the latest best-sellers. Other than her son, who rarely came around, she considered us her family. Mom and me.

But I'd never made it past Shilpa's entry in all the years we'd lived next door. I guess I never really needed to. Once I'd mentioned it to my mom, and she told me Shilpa suffered from severe anxiety and to leave it alone. The way she said it, quiet-like, told me it was something serious and to mind my own business. So, I never pursued it.

"I just wanted to check on you," I said. "Make sure you're doing okay through all of this."

She clutched my forearm and peered at me. Like she needed to say something. But when I thought she would, she'd dart a look at Uncle Angel, her lips pressed tight. The three of us stood in silence on the porch, my uncle using the tip of his loafer to nudge the potted plant.

"It'd help if you watered it," he said, but shut up once I elbowed him.

Shilpa ignored him, speaking directly to me. "I need to speak with Mireya." Her fingers locked in a vice-grip around my forearm. "Alone."

"What the hell? What do you mean *alone*?" Uncle Angel said. "Does it have to do with Ana María's disappearance? If you know something, Shilpa, you need to tell us. *Both* of us. And the police. No time for games here. We have to find my sister before it's too late."

Shilpa lifted her chin. A debate seemed to be taking place inside her head. She glanced my way again, this time questioning, and I nodded my agreement with him. Anything she had to say to me, she could share in front of him. If she knew anything, anything at all, that could help Mom, I wanted both of us to hear it.

She opened her mouth, but paused, her look directed over my uncle's shoulder. A woman walking a dog approached on the sidewalk out front, waving as she and her pooch passed. Shilpa waited until the woman was well past us before she cleared her throat.

"Two men have been following her. That's what she told me three days ago. She'd seen the same men in a car parked outside the grocery store, and then again about a block from the school. Each time she took precautions to make sure they hadn't followed her home." Shilpa said. "I told her to report it to the police, and she assured me she would. But, now, I know that she did not."

"Two? Why didn't you tell the police? What did they look like? Did she say?" Uncle Angel grabbed Shilpa's shoulder and barked questions at her. "Did she describe them to you? What kind of car were they driving? Did she say the color? Big or small? A license plate number?"

"No!" Shilpa recoiled from his touch. "No, no, no. She asked me not to tell anyone, made me swear that I would not. She didn't know who they were. And she did not say anything about the car," she cried. "I didn't think to ask about that. I wish I had, but I didn't."

She buried her face in trembling hands. Her entire body began to silently shake. I took her back in my arms and rocked her as she cried, her tears dampening my shirt.

"Okay, okay. Tell me this. Was she seeing anyone—a boyfriend, maybe?" Uncle Angel asked, a forced gentleness to his voice.

"She never—mentioned that to me—" Shilpa said between sobs. She wiped her wet face with a sleeve. "She didn't say it—but she was planning—something—some way to address whatever was going on—I'm sure of it. I could tell—by the way she acted. But—she wouldn't tell me anything. Her face—I could see—she looked so frightened. And then I saw the TV today— that video." Her crying intensified, but she managed to say, "Why did they—why would they—do this to her? I'm afraid they'll—she doesn't deserve this."

The frozen image of my mother on the surveillance video popped into my head, yet again. I knew where Shilpa was coming from. Red spots flared in my vision.

Yeah, I understood exactly what she meant. That look of pure terror in Mom's eyes just before the two men had dragged her away. It was permanently etched on my brain, no matter how forcefully I tried to push it away. But I didn't know how to protect her from that horror, and even if I did, I didn't know if I could save her before it was too late. If it wasn't already.

CHAPTER 9

Five Days Missing

The past two nights I've been plagued by nightmares about Mom, that frozen video image of her terrified face haunting me. The whites of her eyes. Shadowy figures dragging her away. I reach for her, call out, a rage burning throughout. I try to lunge at the moving shadows pulling her away, but I'm helpless. My feet stay cemented to the ground, as they throw her into a car and speed away, everything fading to black. Then, I'm wandering in a pasture, my bloody hands covered in thorns, as I scramble over mounds of rocky soil, through patches of cactus and shards of bones scattered as far as I can see. A constant howling wind morphs into the sound of my screams. Or maybe they're her screams? That possibility torments me even more.

Tonight, I woke up whimpering, my face soaked in either tears or sweat, I don't know which, with the blankets twisted around my arms and legs, a panic crushing my chest. I struggled to catch my breath, as the horror hit me again and again. Trapped—and desperate. That's how I've felt since her abduction.

This morning was the same drill. It was almost three o'clock when I finally tired of the pretense of sleep. I eased myself out of bed and shuffled toward the kitchen for water.

Some nights my uncle has heard me and gotten up, too, but not this morning. Probably because he was passed out. Before I'd gone to bed last night, he'd sat at the dining room table, hunched over a pile of file folders, sipping from a large glass of bourbon. I wondered what he had in the folders, but when I asked, he said it was work-related and he couldn't say. I'd smelled the liquor on him when I hugged him goodnight. It seeped through his pores like perspiration. God knows how much he'd had to drink.

His empty glass was in the kitchen sink and a half-full bottle sat on the counter. I opened the liquor and sniffed the amber liquid, wrinkling my nose, then screwing the cap back on tight. It brought back a bad memory. I'd been drunk once before at a party my sophomore year. It was trash can punch spiked with some kind of rocket fuel, and I gulped down two cups like it was flavored water. Then it hit. That topsy-turvy-feeling left me clinging to the hallway, as I zig-zagged toward the bathroom. Once I'd locked the door and slid down the wall, my butt planted on the cold tile, my mind turned to total mush, as I repeatedly smacked numb lips together to make sure they were still there. Then I promptly blacked out. About an hour later, my friends pounded on the door. Not only had I freaked them out, but I'd scared myself, too. After that, I decided liquor wasn't my jam.

I walked to my uncle's room where his door was slightly ajar. I eased it open wider, so I could hear him better. A sputtering of snores ricocheted inside. I quietly shut it and sprinted to the kitchen table and the heap of police files there, disregarding the nagging in the back of my brain that I was betraying his trust. Not to mention possibly breaking the law. I flipped through the first file on top. It was an incident report from the bank. Not much there that I hadn't already learned from the video surveillance.

The next one was filled with about twenty mugshots with information sheets stapled to each one. The guys looked like bad news. Some had gang-related, grim reaper tattoos on their necks. Most of them had that same flat, lifeless look in their eyes. I gasped, an icy finger of dread traced down my spine, one vertebra at a time. Was I looking at one of the men who took my mother? Or both? Why was Uncle Angel looking at these creeps as potential suspects? Based on what I read about them, they mostly belonged to a criminal organization based in El Paso, not Dallas, that ran drugs and sex trafficking for a cartel. The gang was apparently making a name for itself across the country. But what was the connection between them and a teacher in the North Dallas suburbs? Mom was a boring middle school math teacher, a major nerd by her own admission, not a drug mule or whatever.

Or was she? She'd been keeping bank accounts secret from me, it appeared. And she had called in sick to work the other day when she hadn't been ill, and instead had wound up at an ATM she wasn't supposed to be at. Was it possible I didn't know as much about her as I had thought?

I'd once read about cartels hiring suburban women to run drugs across the border, since they passed through inspections more easily, looking less likely to be hauling illegal substances than the usual suspects. Paid them big money, too, if I remembered the news story correctly. And there was the money in those bank accounts I couldn't explain to police. I mean, where did all that cash come from? But wait a minute. That wasn't the case here. Mom running drugs? No way. Absolutely not. That was a ridiculous thought. She hated drugs. I couldn't count the number of lectures she'd given me through the years about avoiding them. Plus, her brother was a DEA agent. She wouldn't do that to him. That would be a stupid move—and Mom wasn't dumb. Besides, when would she have time to run drugs anyway? I mean, she almost never took trips, and never without me.

I flipped through other files, but nothing else jumped out. I kept coming back to the mugshots and profiles of the gang members. I jotted down their names on a piece of paper along with notes about their specific cases. I ripped the paper from my spiral, folded it up and slipped it under my bra strap. I'd get online and see what I could find out about these guys. What were we all missing? Did Mom know any of these losers? I needed more information. Apparently, my uncle thought it was important enough to read up on them, even though he wasn't telling me shit. I couldn't really fathom a connection, but I'd find a way to check it out. I'd figure it out without him.

I needed to connect dots. So far, I had nothing but secret bank accounts that made zero sense. But someone had taken her the other morning. And if she'd been followed, like she'd told Shilpa, the douchebags who'd abducted her had been tracking her. It wasn't random. What had she gotten herself into and why wouldn't she let me know about it? Or my uncle, who could have helped her?

I'm not a hunter by nature. Truth is, I can't stand the entire concept of catching and caging living creatures, much less killing them. Too brutal for me. But this was different. I had to help Mom, to save her if I could. The little I knew about hunters (mostly from the National Geographic channel) was they couldn't successfully pursue a predator until they found out every detail that they could about them. Their everyday habits, their needs, their desires.

Grabbing a glass of water and my laptop, I plopped down on the sofa, taking a long swallow before sliding the piece of paper out. I wrapped a fluffy blanket tight around my shoulders and settled in. I had lots of work to do. I googled each name, pulling up various news stories and criminal charges in different Texas counties. My bottom lip dangled lower and lower with each search. Sheesh. These guys were *way* scary. The charges varied from armed robbery to distribution of illegal substances to prostitution and murder. And the gang they were involved with? Holy crap. It had been connected to police shootings, beheadings of rival gang members, massive drug deals, human trafficking across the border. The list of criminal acts went on. I gulped hard, then downed the rest of my water.

"What are you doing?"

I jumped at my uncle's voice, spitting water across the laptop keyboard.

"What the hell!" I yelled, scrambling to mop it up and slam down the laptop screen before he could see what I was up to.

"It's five in the morning. All okay?" He narrowed his bloodshot gaze at me, ruffling the back of his head with both his hands. He looked bedraggled, and his hair, usually slicked back, stuck up at odd angles.

"Well?"

"Well—what?" I asked, hugging the laptop to my chest.

"What are you doing? You're never up this early."

"I am now. Couldn't sleep. Thought I'd work on a research paper for my lit class. It's due in a few days. I'm missing a lot of school, you know," I said, shrugging, the lie popping so easily from my lips. "What about you? Did you get any sleep?"

"Not much." He rubbed at his temples, then vigorously scratched at the stubble darkening his cheeks and chin. "But that's to be expected."

He moved to the kitchen sink, turned on the faucet, and splashed his face a few times. He patted himself dry with a hand towel.

"You hungry?" He asked over his shoulder, as he opened the fridge, grabbing a carton of eggs and container of butter, placing them both on the counter. Then he opened a cabinet, clanging pans together before he found the one he wanted. I bit my lips, wishing he would go back to bed. I needed to get back to my digging without him around.

He cracked an egg into a bowl, then slung open a drawer, taking a spoon and fishing out bits of eggshells. Then he cracked another. And another.

"Sure, I could eat," I said, although I wasn't hungry at all. I forced myself up and started a pot of coffee for us. I needed fuel.

It would take a lot of energy to do what needed to be done, I thought, giving him a fake sleepy smile. He returned the half-hearted grin, as he stirred the eggs in the pan.

"It's going to be okay," he said, as he shook salt and pepper over our breakfast. "I know this feels overwhelming right now, but we'll figure it out, okay?"

"Yeah. We will," I said with certainty, glancing away so he wouldn't see the fire that I knew burned in my eyes.

My mind began spinning. The adrenaline was back, zinging along as my synapses fired and neurons bounced about. Sometimes harrowing circumstances turned people into something they wouldn't be under normal conditions. And it seemed mine was pushing me to become the unwilling hunter. If that was what I had to do to save her, then so be it. I recalled the flatness of those gazes in the mugshots, and an intense fear gripped my heart. Could I really do this? Or was it insane to even think it? But then I saw the image of my mom's face in the surveillance video, and within an instant, my fear transformed into a scorching anger, smoldering within.

I poured a cup of coffee for my uncle, and then one for me, careful to keep my hands steady and eyes averted. I wanted to ask him questions about the files, but I knew I couldn't. He wouldn't tell me anything, anyway. That was certain. He'd tell me it was too dangerous for me to know, or something along those lines. He'd be pissed if he knew what I planned to do behind his back, say it was stupid, or whatever. But at that moment, I couldn't care less what he thought. All I cared about was keeping her alive. Without her, I didn't think I could make it. The harsh truth was this—her survival equaled my survival.

CHAPTER 10

Five Days Missing

I'd watched enough nature programs on television as a kid to know predators had different ways of hunting their prey. Some ran straight at them, full throttle, isolating and overtaking the weakest of the herd. Others camouflaged themselves, blending into surroundings before they'd strike without warning. Some stalked silently, tracking at a distance, taking their time, waiting for the most opportune moment for the kill. And there were those who set traps. That last group was me. I needed to set a trap, but I couldn't do it without finding out as much as I could about Mom's past and her possible connection to the men in the police reports.

I'd called Shilpa a few hours earlier, and Cici had dropped me off so no one would report back to my uncle that I had been out. He'd given strict orders for me to stay put at his house. As I slipped through Shilpa's backyard gate, she hovered at the door, silently motioning me inside. I'd expected we would sit on the patio furniture as we talked; I couldn't believe she was letting me in. She bolted the back door behind me and turned for a hug.

"It's so good to see you, my dear. I've been sick with worry." She stepped back to look at me. "Are you taking care of yourself? Are you eating properly at your uncle's house? It doesn't look like it. You look exhausted, child. I can't imagine what this is doing to you."

"You, too," I said, as I took in the dark smudges under her eyes. She looked so frail. I wondered when she'd eaten last.

Since I'd never been inside, I paused to glance around at what would normally serve as the kitchen nook. I caught my breath. Stacks of magazines and newspapers towered toward the ceiling, and boxes overflowing with recyclables and God-knows-what-else lined the wall. They were stacked so high and closely together that the narrow pathways in between looked like roadways tunneled through mountains.

Shilpa looked around, too, her face turning a warm pink. She ducked her head. "My apologies for the mess. I've been working on, uh, organizing some things."

I gulped. So, this must have been the secret my mom carried for her best friend and why she'd defended Shilpa's unusual behavior whenever I asked about it. This was why no one was allowed inside her home, except my mother. Maybe it was the reason for the strained relationship with her son, too? I didn't know for sure. One thing was clear, though. I would have never guessed this woman, always immaculately put together on the outside, was a hoarder.

But, so what? We all carried our own baggage, right? Maybe some baggage was more visible than others. I was learning that from my mom, who had hidden much more than I'd ever imagined. For all I knew, it might be even more baggage than Shilpa apparently carried within these walls.

"No worries, there's no mess. Boxes don't bother me," I said to Shilpa, squeezing her shoulder. "If you'd feel more comfortable, we can go outsi—"

"No, no," she said, quickly. "I don't feel safe out there. Not since—"

"Right. Me either," I said. "Thanks for letting me come over. I really needed to talk with you face-to-face."

"I'm so glad you're here," she said. "I've made us chai. Do you want a cup while we visit? I put out shortbread cookies, too. Your favorite, if I remember correctly."

"That would be great," I said with a forced grin, even though I hadn't had much of an appetite since mom went missing. "I can't believe you remembered my favorite cookies."

"Of course, I do. Your mom always bought multiple boxes when the Girl Scouts came around, knocking on doors," she said, with a sad laugh, waving me to follow. We moved through the cramped tunnels of her house until we came to the living room with warm lamps, plump chairs, one of those old-fashioned stereo consoles, and a large television mounted above the fireplace. Paintings of villages, presumably in India, adorned the walls, along with a dated portrait of Shilpa and her late husband, which looked to be taken on their wedding day. Her son's photo from college graduation was on a side table, as well as a photo of my mom, Shilpa and myself (all of us laughing,) which had been taken a few years back at one of our cookouts. We were her family, too, and she was missing someone precious to her, just as I was.

"So, what is the reason for the secrecy tonight?" Shilpa asked as she poured our hot tea into mugs. She grabbed a cookie off the plate, before nudging it toward me. She nibbled at it, then reached for the mug, blowing on it before she sipped.

"Anything new from the police? Please tell me you're not here about bad news," she said, her voice slightly breaking, as she cradled the mug in her hands. She peered at me through wisps of steam. "Did they find something? Is that why you've come?"

"No, no, that's not why I'm here. There's nothing, yet." I shook my head, staring down into my own cup. If my mom had told anyone *anything* about her life besides me, it would be Shilpa. I carefully placed the untouched tea on the table and looked at her.

"Shilpa, you and Mom are close, right? Best friends?"

"Of course," she said. "The best of friends. Like sisters, even. I'd do anything for her. Or for you."

I scooted closer to the edge of my seat.

"I need you to tell me what you know about her past. Like anything out-of-the-ordinary that you might remember her mentioning over the years. Whatever she may have told you, even if it was something she didn't want you to share with me, it's important," I said. "Did she ever say anything about any—er, criminal types—like gang members she may have known when she was a young girl? Like maybe a classmate or a neighbor or a family member? Did she ever mention anything about living in El Paso?"

"El Paso? Your mom wasn't from El Paso. She was born and raised in New Mexico—but you already know that." Shilpa said, her forehead scrunched. "What's this about, Mireya?"

I shrugged. I couldn't tell her what I'd found in Uncle Angel's files, especially since I wasn't sure about any connections. Plus, I wasn't supposed to be snooping through police files. Could my uncle get in trouble for having them at his house? I didn't know, but I didn't want to risk it.

"Do you trust me, Shilpa?"

"Yes, of course, I do. But I don't understand the direction of your questioning." She put down her tea, her mouth a flat line. "Criminals and gangs? Really? Your mother would never associate with the likes of those types. You know that. She's one of the most upstanding individuals I've ever known."

I nodded. That's how I felt, too, but there must be some reason my uncle was looking at criminal histories of gang members and had circled names in red.

"Look, I have reason to believe she was hiding something from me. Something really dark. But you may already know that, right?"

I saw it—a flash of pain on her face—before she steadied her features. My gut had been right. She knew something. My mom had shared something with her, but what was it?

"It's possible Mom has been hiding something serious, details from her past, and it may be connected to why those two men where following her—why they took her." I leaned even closer toward Shilpa, my hands grasped together to keep them from trembling. "I don't know what's been going on with her, or what she's been hiding, but I do know if she told anyone about it, it would be you."

She bowed her head.

"Whatever she may have told you, even if it seems like it doesn't matter, please tell me. Even if she asked you not to say anything, it could be the difference in finding her alive," I said, my voice bordering on a cry. "Please. It might lead us to her. *I need to find her.*"

Shilpa pinched the bridge of her nose. We both sat in silence for a few beats. She finally looked at me.

"I promised her I wouldn't say anything unless something happened to her," she said, in an uneven whisper. "She made me swear."

"What? But something *has* happened to her. She has been missing for five days—almost six. She might be hurt—or worse. Please. Tell me. I'm begging you."

"Forgive me, Ana María," she murmured to the ceiling, followed by a deep sigh. She stared at the hands in her lap, sitting perfectly still for what seemed like eternity. Then her gaze moved up to mine.

"I don't think you understand. I don't know what you're referring to, I mean about her past before I met her. What I'm talking about has to do with what's been going on with her recently," she said, standing up from the chair. "Stay right there. I need to show you something."

Shilpa walked slowly from the room. I reached for my mug and took a long sip. Boxes scraped against the floor in a nearby room, and then I heard something crash to the ground.

"Everything okay?" I called out, half-rising from my seat.

"I'm fine," she called back, out of breath. "Be right there."

She came back into the room carrying a small plastic bin in her arms. She sat down and placed it on the floor next to her chair.

"What's in there?" I asked, eyeing the manila envelopes and sheets of paper I could see through the clear plastic.

Shilpa bit at the corner of her lip. She placed a protective hand on top of the bin, before finally speaking.

"If you feel like your mom has been hiding something lately—well, unfortunately, you're correct. And it is dark," she said, her voice raspy. "But I don't believe it has anything to do with her abduction."

"You don't know that. Tell me what's going on," I said, reaching for the bin. "This might point me in the right direction, help me figure out who took her!"

Shilpa shook her head, as she slid the bin over to me.

"I wish it did, dear, but no."

I fumbled with the lid and grabbed at the first item on top. It was a manila envelope with the word "Will" and "Insurance Papers" written on the front in my mom's small handwriting. I opened and pulled out the papers. After scanning them, I tossed them aside. Next was a small daily planner I hadn't seen before, and I quickly flipped through it. Since January, she'd been logging appointments with a person named

Dr. Reynolds. *Who was that?* There also were appointment times jotted down for imaging tests and blood work as recent as two weeks ago. *What the hell?*

"I don't get it." I looked up at Shilpa. "Who's this Dr. Reynolds person? And why didn't I know about these tests? This doesn't make sense."

Shilpa reached for the final item in the box and placed it on the table in front of me.

"Dr. Reynolds is an oncologist," she said, motioning to the leather-bound journal she had laid in front of me. Her eyes watered. "Ana María is sick. It's an aggressive type of cervical cancer."

The last word turned my blood to ice water. I could barely move my lips to speak.

"What? You're sure?" I sat back, shocked and confused. "Cancer? But why wouldn't she tell me?"

She leveled sad eyes on mine.

"She didn't want you to worry about her. She wanted to take care of things before she discussed it with you. She stored all the paperwork here, so you wouldn't find it," she said quietly, placing her hand on my knee. "Please don't be angry with her. She was trying to protect you. Make sure you'd be taken care of if anything happened."

"Taken care of?" I palmed my forehead, struggling to comprehend the latest twist in my mother's secrets. "I'm tired of being lied to or not told things—for my protection. Tell me—what exactly is going on? I need details. Help me make sense of this, because from where I'm sitting right now, this is seriously messed up."

"Oh, God. How do I say this? It isn't fair to you," Shilpa said, her features contorting into misery. She wrapped her arms tight around her chest. "Your mother doesn't have long to live, Mireya. It's the cancer—it's terminal."

"What do you mean terminal? Stop. Back up. There must be treatments for it, right? Chemo? Radiation? We could try something else, anything, like experimental trials in Europe or maybe we could get her into M.D. Anderson in Houston or something like that. Right?"

Her chin dropped to her chest, tears leaking down gaunt cheeks.

"No," I said, shaking my head. A heaviness consumed my entire body, a gravity that shoved me deeper into the chair. "I don't believe it. I just don't."

I buried my face in my hands, my mind reeling from what Shilpa had revealed. On top of all the other shit going on, Mom was dying? From an aggressive form of cancer? Is that what she was saying? How could Mom not tell me she was ill? Did she believe I was still that little kid who had to be shielded from the ugly world? Or maybe she'd assumed I wasn't capable of taking care of her? I struggled with my mother's logic, or lack of it, while resentment and sadness played tug-of-war with my thoughts. I still had no answers about her past or possible connection to those men in the police files. How could she do this to me? Leave me with these unknowns, an illness I was ignorant of, bank accounts flush with cash, and me floundering to make sense of a person I loved with every ounce of my being, but maybe didn't fully understand.

"How long?" I finally asked. "How long did the doctors give her?"

Shilpa sobbed softly into her hands, struggling to spit out the words.

"Shilpa? How long does she have?"

"Maybe a year? Possibly three," she finally got out. "She said they couldn't be exact."

Sorrow finally won the battle in my brain, as the leather journal on the table caught my eye. I grabbed it and clutched it to my chest as I began to sob—a full-on ugly cry—and Shilpa tried her best to comfort me. Maybe Mom had left an explanation within its pages. Maybe she'd tell me why she'd kept the truth from me—from the one who loved her most.

I had to find her. Knowing she was sick, I had to do everything in my power to bring her home, make her comfortable, let her know I was there to care for her every step of the way. She didn't have to protect me anymore. It was my turn. I would do whatever it took to protect her.

CHAPTER 11

Five Days Missing

Cici picked me up in the alley behind Shilpa's house after I'd texted. As I fell into her car, she turned down the '90s grunge music blasting from her playlist. Normally, I would have cranked the volume even louder, but I wasn't in the mood. Not after hearing what Shilpa had said about my mom.

"Holy crap," Cici said, with a pointed look before starting the car, "you look wrecked, babe." She carefully navigated the alley, shooting curious glances my way, before turning off the music. She tossed a handful of tissues from her console, which I gratefully pressed against my face.

"Wanna talk about it?"

I couldn't speak without choking up, so I shook my head no. A throbbing started at the base of my neck and punched its way up the back of my skull.

"Got it." She breaked at the red light, flipped down the visor, then smeared lip balm on her lips before clearing her throat.

"So, Luka has been texting me constantly for updates. Said you haven't been answering him the past few days? Such a boy, right?" She puckered her lips in the mirror before flicking the visor up. "I let him know you'd been busy and that search you went on the other day kinda freaked you out. I also told him to get over himself. You need space. But he says he wants to see you, just to lay eyes on you, so I told him you were staying at your uncle's. Hope that's okay."

"Yeah, sure," I mumbled. "Whatever."

Cici turned left, driving toward Uncle Angel's place. I couldn't believe Luka had been texting me. Like constantly. A week ago, I would have been screaming with joy, maybe doing a seriously goofy happy dance. But right now, I could hardly summon the energy to brush my teeth. I was overwhelmed, as in one hundred percent emotionally wrung out. It was nothing against him. He'd been great, sending me supportive messages and offering to help anyway he could. I just didn't know how to act normal since Mom had been taken—even around someone I happened to like as much as him.

We rode in silence a few minutes more before Cici spoke again.

"Listen, you seem even more upset than before, which blows me away, considering I didn't think that was possible. You need to talk about what you're going through. I'm telling you that as a friend, and because I love you. Like my therapist always tells me, you can't keep all this bottled inside—it's too much shit," she said, as I sagged deeper in the passenger seat. "Was Shilpa any help with whatever you needed from her?"

I looked out the window, as everything blurred past. I hadn't told Cici about the files at Uncle Angel's, either. How could I? I still had no clue what anything meant or why my mom was targeted at the ATM that morning or by whom. And now this horrible news.

"I'm here for anything. You know that, right?"

"I know," I said, still staring out the window. How could I tell her that not only was my mom missing, but she also had incurable cancer? That she was either dead or being tortured at the hands of two unknown men, and, oh, by the way, she was also staring into the abyss of a monster disease. How messed up was that, anyway?

"Okay, dude. We need to shake things up here. Literally. These are desperate times, and we need to do something that feels ordinary, even if it's a little thing," Cici said, as she whipped into the Sonic parking lot and pulled in to order.

Other teenagers were milling around at outside tables. Cici rolled down the window, filling the car with shrieks of laughter from a group of teens eating at a one of the outdoor tables. A girl and a boy were throwing French fries at each other, giggling, obviously flirting. It had been less than a week since Mom went missing, but it seemed like ages ago since I had last laughed like that. I wasn't sure I'd ever remember what it had felt like to be a regular high school kid on a Friday night, hanging out at the Sonic. Wistfully, I watched them, feeling like a senior citizen, instead of one of them.

"Want your usual 'shitstorm special'?"

"Sure." I attempted a smile. Cici was trying hard to cheer me up, but she had no idea of the level of shitstorm, yet. My chin sunk to my chest, as I dabbed at my watery eyes. Deflated. My body felt like all the oxygen had been sucked out.

She laid on the large, red intercom button, and a voice answered over the speaker.

"We need two large banana shakes. Oh, and two Frito pies. No onions, please!" She smirked at me, as I raised my eyebrows. "What? You need to eat, and so do I! Besides, banana shakes are required for crap times like these."

A lump rose in my throat as I stared at my best friend. Maybe she did understand the level of shitstorm in which I was swimming, even if she didn't know all the depressing details.

Exhaustion, or maybe resignation, pulled me heavier against the seat. The stress of these past days—I was sick of it all. Of searching for bodies out in the middle of fucking nowhere, never knowing if we'd stumble over a dead person. Of not knowing whether my mom was alive. Of Uncle Angel's odd behavior. Of Shilpa's revelation about the cancer.

I just wanted to go back to that morning I last saw Mom and stop her from going to that damn ATM. I wanted to carry her books for her to the car and eat cold pizza with her later that night, after she dragged herself home from a long day with students. I wanted to tell her she didn't have to hide the cancer diagnosis—to keep that daunting secret to herself—and make sure she knew I would drop everything, even college, to care for her. Whatever she needed. I'd cook for her, drive her to doctor's appointments, work puzzles with her, and do all the things she had done for me my entire life. That she didn't always have to be the one who took care of everything this time. That I could be strong for her. If only I could go back to that morning, knowing what I knew now.

The weight of all the secrets and unknowns wedged inside my throbbing head. I watched the carhop skate to Cici's side and pass our items through the window. Cici put the shake in the cupholder next to me and handed me a Frito pie. I placed it on the dashboard.

"Sure you don't want to talk about it?" Cici said, shoveling a bite of chili pie into her mouth. "C'mon—" she chomped loudly, taking a noisy sip of her shake, "—spill it, bestie. But only if you want to."

"Well, I'm not even sure how to explain it all," I said, a few beats of silence following. "So, on top of everything else, it looks like my mom is really sick. She never told me any of this—she only told Shilpa. Like, she didn't trust me with it, you know?"

Cici stopped chewing, cocked her head at me, while still cupping the Frito pie dish in front, the plastic fork suspended in front of her mouth.

"Sick? What do you mean sick? Like how?"

I drew a shaky breath and hugged myself, shivering despite the eighty-something-degree temperature outside. "As in battling cancer. Like the terminal kind of sick."

"Oh my god." Cici set her chili pie on the dash, her eyes bulging. "Are you sure? Maybe Shilpa got it wrong."

I looked at her and shook my head, the same way Shilpa had looked at me an hour earlier.

"Mom had test results and other stuff stored at Shilpa's. Plus, this," I said, reaching for the journal and planner I'd shoved in my backpack. I'd left the rest of the stuff with Shilpa to keep it safe. "I'll go through it later. Right now, I just—"

"I'm so sorry, girl." Cici hugged me tightly, speaking into my hair. "I don't even know what to say. My head is exploding. How are you keeping your shit together? This is too much for one person to take. Seriously."

"There's more, but you can't tell anyone, because I'm not even supposed to know," I said in a small voice. I pulled away and tried not to break down again. "I think Uncle Angel's looking into some kind of gang connection to Mom's abduction."

"Gang? You mean like a gang initiation thing? I've heard they do shit like that, like shoot people in a drive-by to prove they're tough, or whatever. Does Uncle Angel think your mom was in the wrong place at the wrong time?"

I grabbed the chili pie in front of me, using my fork to swirl chili and corn chips together in a figure-eight pattern. It smelled delicious, but my stomach lurched. I carefully returned it to the dash.

"I think he thinks there's more to it than that. The files of the guys he was looking at were hardcore criminal types with lots of arrests in connection with an El Paso gang I've never heard of. I looked it up online, and it's not good. The guys in his files were scary as hell, Cici. Like some of them—well, they killed people. Like in really gruesome ways."

"Okay, but your mom's a nerdy math teacher—no offense, because she's tough, too—but not someone who'd hang with murders. No way. Plus, she's the person who'd call the cops if someone ran a stop sign."

"I know, I know. But Uncle Angel must know something we don't, because he's digging into those guys." I rolled down my window to get fresh air. "Seriously, Cici, he has no idea I looked through those files. You really can't say anything to anybody. He'd be pissed if he found out I was poking through official police files."

"Got it." Cici's face was pale. "None of this makes sense, though."

"No, it doesn't," I said. "You know, a couple days ago, I basically accused him of being involved."

"What? You did not." She leaned back in the driver's seat. "Do you seriously believe that?"

"No. But something's off with him, you know. I mean, I know he's trying to find her, but it feels like he's hiding important information, too. Like something more than mug shots. That's what my gut is telling me, but I don't know what it could be. Do you think it's possible he's somehow connected to her going missing?"

"Not a chance, babe. You three are the tightest family circle I know."

"Yeah," I said, with a deep sigh. "I'm being paranoid, but see, that's where my mental state is. He told me I'm losing it, and he's probably right. I need to get my head straight."

Through the windshield I could see the high schoolers playfully pushing one another. I figured they were freshmen or sophomores, younger than us.

"You wanna know the worst part, the part I can't seem to forgive myself for?" I whispered. "It's how I treated her. Mom, I mean."

"How you what? None of this is your fault, Mireya!"

"No, not that. But I watched her leave that morning, you know. Saw her juggling all her papers and books and crap, but I didn't open the car door for her. I mean, why? Looking back, I was such a jerk. It would have been a simple thing to do." I closed my eyes. "That's the last image I have of her before those assholes took her. Her struggling with stuff, things falling, and me watching, bugged that she was taking so long, but still not bothering to help her open the damn door. I'm a horrible daughter—it's no wonder she didn't tell me she was sick."

We sat in silence. Me too numb to cry much anymore, and Cici apparently processing all that I'd unloaded on her in a few short minutes.

"Okay. That's enough," Cici said. She gathered the half-eaten chili pie and tossed it into a bag. "Want me to tell you something I remember? A memory I have?"

She didn't give me a chance to respond.

"You gave an oral report in seventh-grade social studies about the most influential person in your life. Remember who that was? Your *mom*. It was a gutsy move in junior high, I mean most of us were naming Michelle Obama, Taylor Swift or Lady Gaga. Parents weren't exactly the cool picks, you know?"

"Remember when Ms. Reeder asked you to give a deeper explanation of why your mom was so influential to you? Remember what you said? Because I do," she said, quietly. "You told Ms. Reeder, 'Because my mom believes in me. She believes I can move mountains, if I try hard enough, and I know she knows what she's talking about, because she can move them, too.'"

"Okay." I squinted at Cici. I wasn't following. "So? Why bring that up?"

"Because if the cliché fits?" Cici said. "Your mom was right—you *can* move mountains. I've known you for what, like six years, and I've seen you do it. Remember that time you put together an enormous bake sale to raise money for the library when the school board cut its budget to almost zero? Remember calling out Jackson Jones, Mr. Wannabe Popular, for bullying that one kid for being gender fluid? You stood up in front of the entire class and called him a dickhead, even though you got detention for cussing. It was beautiful!"

"I can list more, but my point is, you're fierce. Just like your mom," she said, swiping my untouched Frito pie and chucking it in the bag. "She raised you to be a badass nerd, just like her. She taught you to be smart and tough and to move fucking mountains."

I swallowed hard as I listened. Mom did raise me to be all those things. The pounding in my head started to recede. Slightly.

"I'm guessing if she didn't tell you about the cancer, she had good reasons, even if we don't know what they are," Cici said, finishing with a slurp. She pointed at me with the straw of her milkshake. "So enough with the pity party about that morning. Cut yourself some slack. You had no idea what was going to happen at that ATM, and yes, if you could go back, you'd open the car door for her and not be a jerk."

"But, here's the deal. You can't go back, only forward toward those fucking mountains." She turned on the car, the engine rumbling as she backed out of the spot. "So, my question for you is this: What's the first step you need to take in order to get those mountains moving?"

Damn. My mouth hung open, as I stared at my best friend who'd just delivered a film-worthy motivational speech. She was right. I didn't have time to feel sorry for myself anymore. I needed to find out who had my mom and why. I motioned to the journal in my lap, in response to Cici's question.

"Then let's get started," she said, all business, as she glanced in the rearview mirror before turning the steering wheel. "I'm here to help however you need me. I've always got your back."

"By the way—DAMN," I said, drawing out the word as I side-eyed her.

"Damn?"

"That was a kickass little speech you just gave, my friend. You killed it!"

She laughed, keeping her gaze on the road ahead.

"But, seriously, thank you for being you," I said to her profile. We whipped onto the busy street, headed back to my uncle's house.

"Anytime, dude." She tilted her head and grinned at me. "Now finish that banana shake. You're gonna need the energy."

CHAPTER 12

Five Days Missing

Uncle Angel wasn't home when Cici dropped me off, which was a good thing, since he'd be furious that I'd snuck over to Shilpa's. She'd offered to stay with me until he got home, but I wanted to be alone. Before Cici would leave, she made me go through the house, turning on lights one-by-one in each room, then she reluctantly waved goodbye and drove away.

But now that I was on my own, the silence of the house suffocated me. It was hard to breathe within these walls. I thought about turning on the television for sound but tossed the remote back on the coffee table before using it. I couldn't handle any news updates about Mom. The reports usually included the replay of that damned surveillance video, which shredded my heart every time I watched it. The physical pain of it was excruciating.

I didn't know what to do with myself. I itched all over—my scalp, my arms and stomach, even my eyeballs— and my nerves quivered inside. The bitterness, rage, betrayal—but mostly the fear—simmered like a toxic stew underneath my skin. I flung myself on the couch and pulled a pillow against my chest, shouting profanities into it, screaming as loud as I could until my vocal cords hurt. Then I bawled—for my mom and for what she had faced without anyone's help. The abduction. The cancer. It wasn't a pity party—it was more of a release of the poison I could feel clouding behind my eyelids.

I finally calmed down and pulled out Mom's journal, pausing before opening it. I quickly chucked it back into my backpack, petrified to read it just yet. What if there was even more? My emotional bandwidth felt stretched beyond its limits, threatening to come undone. Too much was happening. At any moment, my sanity could give way, and then what use would I be to her? How could I help my mom if I cracked?

I hugged my knees and rocked, listening to the rhythm of my breathing. Cici was right. We needed some normalcy in order to reset. But it seemed impossible to find anything normal in a world where my mom, the strongest person I knew, disappeared at gunpoint in two blinks of an eye. She had to be somewhere, and yet, she wasn't. At least not anywhere that we could locate. Meanwhile, time kept shoving us forward. Each hour meant less of a chance we'd find her alive. My mind recoiled at the thought, refusing to go down that rabbit hole right now.

The phone vibrated in my pocket, but I ignored it. I didn't want to talk to anyone, not in my current crazy state.

Someone knocked loudly on the front door. I startled, then froze in panic. All the lights were on, and whoever it was could probably see movement within. Who would be knocking on the door at ten o'clock at night.? Now I wished Cici had waited with me until Uncle Angel came home. My uncle's recent talk about *danger, danger* kept pinging in my brain. I got to my feet, my knees wobbly, unsure what to do next. Maybe I could bolt for the bathroom and hide in there? I was frustrated that my uncle hadn't invested in a video security system, especially right now. What kind of law enforcement officer didn't have security cameras in his own home? I'd speak to him about it, if I wasn't murdered in the next five minutes.

Knock, knock again. And then the ringing of the doorbell. The phone thrummed in my pocket a second time. I pulled it out and scrolled through texts. The most recent one read: *It's Luka. You in there?*

A huge sigh of relief.

"Coming! Just a second!" I called to him through the door, before scurrying to the living room mirror. I combed fingers through my lank hair and used the bottom of my shirt to dab at red, puffy eyes. There wasn't much I could do.

I peered through the door viewer just to make sure it was him. Despite feeling half-zombie, my heart skipped erratically, as it often did when I saw him. I stood there for a moment, taking him in. Striking dark eyes, framed by long lashes, danced in front of me. I unlocked the door and let him pull me into his arms. It was slightly clumsy, but I didn't mind. He'd never hugged me like this before.

"Hey." He mumbled into my hair.

"Hey," I said, breathing in the piney scent of soap. I pressed my face deeper against his chest.

"I wasn't sure I had the right place. Cici texted this address to me."

He pulled back a little, looking at my face.

"You've been crying," he said softly.

I gave a weak shrug. There was no sense in denying it.

His thumb traced my cheek bone, where a warmth reddened my skin. He cradled the side of my face in his palm. He had never touched me that way. The heat that sparked across my body was the most normal thing I'd felt in days. I wanted to kiss him, and I think he wanted that, too. How easy it would be to lose myself in this new thing. But, realistically, it was a dumb idea. I had more urgent matters to deal with than a first kiss with my crush.

"I've missed you. You didn't return my calls or texts." His face was so close to mine, his look so intense. "I've been climbing the walls. Couldn't sleep. I've been really worried about you."

"I'm sorry—it's been a lot. Too much, really," I said, breaking eye contact. "I've kinda shut down, you know?"

I awkwardly stepped away and led him into the living room. He had an envelope and a notebook that he tossed on the coffee table. We sat down on the couch, shoulder to shoulder.

"No worries. I get it." He turned toward me, his knee resting against mine. "I'm here in whatever way you need. Everyone on the debate team, well, we've been trying to figure out what we can do for you. How can we help?" he said, fidgeting with a loose thread on the seam of his jeans. He looked miserable, like his usual confident self had been left at the front door. "We're all shocked. About your mom, I mean. What happened to her—well, it's beyond messed up."

"Yeah, it is." I gulped. I didn't want to cry in front of him, but the mention of my mom and something about the worried tone of his voice made me feel weepy again. God, I had to pull my shit together. But I wasn't sure I was strong enough.

"Let's not talk about it right now. I'm kinda shaky," I said, inching away. I nervously rubbed my palms against the tops of my thighs. "Tell me what's happening at school. What's going on with graduation?"

I figured that was a safe topic, but then it hit me he'd be leaving for college in San Diego once summer ended. I turned my head away, as tears welled up once more. I bit the inside of my cheek to keep the sadness at bay. It wasn't like we had even gone out or anything, but still, he'd be leaving me soon, too.

"I'm ready, I guess." He shrugged and scratched the side of his neck. "My parents are a pain in the ass, right now, freaking out over the expense of out-of-state tuition. I busted my butt to get scholarships, but it's still expensive. Lots of arguments over the phone and shit, but that's nothing new. Usual communication style. Guess that's why they divorced."

"That's not cool."

"No, it's not, but it's whatever. Life in the Allred clan, yeah?" He smiled hesitantly.

The corner of my lips turned up in a shadow of a smile. I wanted to ask him when he planned to leave for California. Did he know what dorm he'd live in? Who his roommates would be? Normal stuff like that, but I couldn't force myself to do it. It all made me even more melancholy if that were possible. I edged even farther away from him on the couch, aware of the uncomfortable silence that followed.

He reached for the envelope on the table and handed it to me.

"That's a card from the team. They miss you, too," he said quietly. "We all signed it, but you can read it later. Everyone chipped in and got you a gift card. Hope that's okay."

"That's really sweet of y'all." I swallowed hard, looking down at the card in my lap.

"You sure you don't want to talk?"

"There's not a lot to say, except everything's beyond screwed up. I'm trying to figure out a way to help my mom, but I feel so useless, really." My knee bounced up and down, and he laid his hand on top of it to slow it. I didn't feel the heat in his touch this time. Instead, the temperature was near freezing. "It's the waiting that's eating at me, you know? We should have found her by now. Every passing hour—"

I couldn't finish the sentence, but he nodded and sighed. Silence followed.

"I'm not sure what to say," he finally said. I couldn't look at him.

"Nobody does. Not even me," I said, swiping at a rogue tear and standing up suddenly. That trapped feeling was back. I wanted to bolt outside and just keep running. My chest tightened. How I'd gone from sizzling to sub-zero sitting next to him was insane. Maybe crazy *was* my new normal.

But then another feeling slammed into me. *Shame.* Luka reminded me of the secrets I'd been keeping from mom before she went missing, the lie I'd told her during our last conversation, when I said I'd be working late that night on my debate case. How I'd been fibbing about my afterschool activities for more than a month. *Why hadn't I told her the truth, maybe even introduced her to Luka?* She'd been praising me for putting in extra hours for debate class, but, really, I'd been hanging out with my friends and him, hoping for a chance to get closer to him. She would have been so disappointed if she'd known. The last words I'd spoken to her had been a lie.

Everything was a mess. I covered my face with my hands, on the verge of wailing again. Luka jumped up to hold me, but I winced when his arms touched me.

"You okay?" He took a backward step, his hands out front. "What just happened?"

My thoughts spun. None of this was his fault, but I couldn't do this right now. I couldn't be near him. I needed to focus on Mom. I needed to move fucking mountains to find her. No distractions.

"I can't," I whispered, as I uncovered my face.

"You can't what? I'm not following what's happening here." He shook his head in confusion. He looked tired.

"I can't do this right now." My voice sounded unsteady. "I can't be your—your flirtation, or whatever, right now. It's not you. I just—can't."

Luka inched closer but didn't touch me. He shoved his hands in his pockets and looked down, his eyelashes casting shadows on his face.

"I can't pretend to understand what's happening to you. I mean, I can't begin to imagine the hell you're going through." He heaved another sigh. "I wish I could change all this, but that's not possible. You can push me away if that's what you need right now, but you gotta know, I'm not going anywhere. You know I like you, have always liked you. So, whether you're my girlfriend—or just a friend—or whatever, I'm still here for you. Whenever."

Did he say *girlfriend*? If things were different, I'd jump him, wrap myself around him. But they weren't. My mom was missing, maybe even dead, although I didn't want to think about that, and I couldn't deal with romantic feelings right now. I stared at the Adam's apple below the cleft of his chin. I wanted to flee from the painful realization I might never feel Luka's arms around me under normal circumstances. I may never really know anything normal again.

My body swayed with exhaustion. A numbness spread through my brain. I needed sleep. Maybe if I slept, I'd wake up to a world where this nightmare had never happened.

"Thank you for that," I said, my arms wrapped around my chest. "But, listen, my uncle will be home soon, and trust me, he won't be happy if you're here. It's not you, it's just, he'd be angry knowing I let anybody inside. There's just a lot going on right now."

Luka looked like he had something else to say but suddenly changed his mind.

"Got it." He grabbed the notebook off the coffee table and paused at the door. "No matter how messed up this all is, you know you're not alone, right? We're all thinking about you." He paused. "I'm thinking about you."

I gripped the tops of my arms and studied the floor.

"Right," he said, grabbing my shoulder, giving it a quick squeeze, then letting go. "I'll see you. Call or text if you need anything, yeah? I mean it."

"I will. I promise," I said, just above a whisper, still not making eye contact. "And thanks for checking on me."

The door shut quietly behind him. I stood motionless for a few minutes, gathering my wits. I wanted to throw the door open and call him back, but I also knew I needed to keep it shut tight for now. If only things were different. I pressed my cheek against the door's smooth, cold surface, before turning the deadbolt. I made my way to the couch where I curled up in a ball, too numb to cry anymore.

I couldn't move. A heaviness weighted pinned my body down. I wanted my life back. I needed my mom. As I waited for Uncle Angel, exhaustion overtook me. I drifted off and found myself in a dream with Mom. She was climbing a rocky path on the side of what looked like a desert canyon, grabbing onto boulders and scrub brush to pull herself up. She turned back to help me. She glowed from a sheen of sweat, and red dirt covered her hands.

"Mireya," she whispered, a blissful grin spreading across her face, "you are loved." My heart expanded at the happiness emanating from her. I couldn't speak, though I tried. She tenderly grasped my hand, her strong fingers interlacing with mine. Holding her hand felt so real, as did the joy that spread through me.

I woke to Uncle Angel gently shaking me, helping me to my feet, and leading me to bed. I quickly returned to the dream, hearing my mother in that dreamy whisper again. "Remember, mija, you are *never* alone." She let go of my hand, and I fell into a cool, deep blackness. For the first time since she had disappeared, I slept soundly through the night.

Chapter 13

Six Days Missing

J esus stood before me, arms outstretched, palms up, watching with a benevolent, toffee-colored gaze. I sat three rows back in a pew at the church Mom and I had attended since we'd moved here. Before me was a standing sculpture of Jesus, not the real deal, although I had the strong sensation somebody *was* watching me. I ducked my head around, shooting furtive glances in all directions, noticing about twenty people scattered in pews, most of them older folks. Some were on bended knees, their mouths moving silently as their fingers worked strings of rosary beads. Others sat with eyes closed, either praying, meditating, or sleeping. It was tough to tell the difference.

I wrinkled my nose. Maybe I was getting as paranoid as my mother and Uncle Angel. I didn't spot anyone looking my way, so I settled back in the hard, wooden pew and soaked up the flickering candlelight from a nearby stand, the colored light high above seeping through stained-glass windows, the gorgeous sculptures of angels adorning the church. This was the place I felt closest to her, especially now. My mom loved it here—the peacefulness of it surrounding her. She'd told me that more than once, but I didn't quite comprehend what she'd meant. Until now.

After days of living in constant chaos and fear of the unknown, I got it. This place must have been a sanctuary for her.

I closed my eyes, allowing myself to visualize her sitting close to me, my head tucked into the nook of her neck and shoulder, something I'd done at Mass since I was a small child. Behind closed eyes, in my personal movie of the two of us, she leaned over and kissed the top of my head. It felt so real, like the dream I'd had of her last night. *I miss you, Mom. Please stay alive until we find you.* I wondered if she could hear me speaking to her, wherever she was. It felt like she could, like she was inches away, gently breathing, the light pressure of her shoulder pressing against my cheek. Goosebumps erupted over my arms as I opened my eyes, half expecting to see her there. But I sat alone, my body slumped against my backpack.

No doubt I was on the verge of losing it. Overwhelmed, worried. So much so, I was feeling a presence beside me that wasn't there, damn near hallucinating. But I couldn't fold, couldn't give into it, even though it'd be easier to dream her back to me. Maintaining focus was more crucial than ever. I had to gather more facts. Try to make sense of the jigsaw puzzle that'd become my life within less than a week. Find the missing pieces that would lead me to her. The police hadn't mentioned anything about a connection to gang members or questioned me about it, so I had a strong feeling Uncle Angel wasn't telling them everything he might know either.

What was he hiding, anyway, and why? Didn't he want to do everything possible to find her? What did he know that the rest of us didn't, and could it lead us to Mom? He'd been so distant the past few days. Distracted, really. Yesterday, he'd made it clear I was to stay put in his house and lock all the doors. I wasn't allowed to go anywhere. He'd even snatched my house keys when I'd mentioned I needed to pick up a few more things from home. His hooded eyes remained guarded. It could be dangerous, he'd told me cryptically, but didn't elaborate, even when I questioned him.

"I'll take you to the house myself, as soon as I can. I promise," he'd said, a sharpness in his tired voice. "Until then, stay here, and don't let anyone in."

Then he'd left, taking all the files stuffed in his laptop bag. He came home sometime after one o'clock in the morning, oblivious to the fact that Cici had driven me to Shilpa's last night, a detail I wouldn't divulge any time soon. I could keep secrets, too.

Did he know Mom had cancer? I wondered, and although I was desperate to find out, I hadn't asked him this morning, because I would have had to reveal my visit with Shilpa. He was looking more haggard each day, and today he seemed more grumpy than usual. Before I said anything about anything to him, I needed to read my mom's journal, something I couldn't emotionally handle last night. Instead, this morning, I told Uncle Angel that I wanted to come here and pray for Mom. He'd narrowed his eyes at me, skeptical, then agreed to drive me and wait outside. He wasn't much for this place, so I knew I'd be safe from him joining me.

I glanced around again, then once more at Jesus, before carefully pulling out the journal, flipping it open, and smoothing down the first page covered in Mom's left-slanted handwriting, as if I could touch her through her written words. I began reading the first entry, dated almost five months ago in January, the words coming to me in her voice:

My Dearest Mireya,

If you're reading this, I'm no longer here. (Shilpa swore to me she wouldn't give you this unless that was the case.) It was not my plan to leave you so soon. Believe me, if given the choice, I would have rather watched you graduate high school and college, watch you become a successful artist or lawyer (you have the mind for both) or whatever you decide to pursue, maybe see you get married and have children of your own (if that's what you want.) All those wonderful milestones I'll miss as your mother. It wounds my soul that I won't get to spend those years with you, see you achieve your heart's desire, but sometimes we're faced with circumstances beyond our control. It's a cliché, I know, but it has often been the case in my life, anyway. This diagnosis is another of those times. Despite it, I have hope I'll get a front row seat to the rest of your life, watching from the other side. I'm not sure how it all works, but I'll always be cheering you on in whatever way I'm allowed.

I need you to understand that I tried to beat the cancer, but since you're reading this, the experimental treatments and therapies must not have been successful. It was a slim chance, but I had to take it. You know that I'd never willingly leave you. I put up a fight, of that you can be certain. It's in my nature, and it's in yours, as well.

Please don't let my death steal hope from you. Hold onto it, even in the bleakest of times. Hope has been one of the greatest gifts I was ever given. It has led me through many challenging moments in my lifetime and gave me the resilience to go on when I wasn't sure where life would lead. Trust me, it will guide you on all your journeys, if you let it, Mireya. (BTW, did you know I chose that name because you were an unexpected miracle in my life? The name has fit you since Day One.)

I'll close for tonight. I'm tired, and writing this is much more difficult than I thought. You'll be home from Cici's soon, and I don't want you to see me upset. I know you'll be disappointed that I didn't tell you about my illness, but I'm not strong enough right now to see your face when I do. I'm not brave enough to tell you many things just yet, things that eventually you'll have to learn, but we can deal with these other issues later, once I've had time to prepare.

I love you and will always be with you.

Mami

P.S.: Always believe. I know you'll move mountains, mija.

I sat bent over the journal, softly sobbing. There were many more entries, but I needed to catch my breath. Hyperventilating in the church wasn't an option. I still didn't get why she hadn't told me she was sick. And what was she referring to when she mentioned "other issues" and she "needed time to prepare?" It made no sense, which I found myself saying a lot lately. All I knew for sure was that we needed to save her from those lunatics and get her the treatment she needed. Maybe the experimental trial and therapies *were* working. We would never know if we didn't get her home soon. I had to move those damned mountains blocking me at almost every step.

I flipped through the rest of the journal, scanning her words. Some of the pages dealt with her treatments, which she apparently had done while I was at school, or at debate tournaments. It explained how pale and worn out she'd looked lately. I should have paid closer attention, but I'd been inside my own head most days. Other pages in the journal dealt with Shilpa being the executor of the will and how she would help get me set for college.

The last entry, dated a few weeks ago, gave me pause:

Mireya,

I'll always be your mami, the one who loves you to the moon and back, times infinity, regardless of what happens. Please remember that, no matter what. You are my miracle. I have loved you since your first breath, that first moment I held you, watching as you opened your eyes and looked around, so curious about the world. Without you, my life would have been empty. Full stop. Whatever I have done, it has been in an effort of giving you the best life possible. I don't mean to write in such a mysterious fashion, but remember what I once said about circumstances? It seems life is throwing some more circumstances at us right now. Me and you. A potentially dangerous situation of which I've tried to shield us from for quite a while. It's too risky for me to explain in writing, but if you should read this, remember what I always told you—sometimes the pieces are right in front of us, we just need to peer into the cracks to find them, no? If you can do that, you'll find the clarity you're most likely looking for right now. Remember that game we used to play—my version of Hide and Seek? Remember you must touch home base first, or you're out. If it has come to that, get to that base as fast as you can. I know you'll figure it out, my smart daughter. I believe in you.

Love, with everything I am,

Mami

I finished the entry, my heart racing. My mind spun in different directions, a buzzing between my ears. *WTF?* Of course, I remembered Hide and Seek, but what was she talking about? Had she hidden something for me to find—something that would bring me "clarity?" What did she mean by "dangerous circumstances?" Had she known someone was coming for her? I was more puzzled than ever, and even more afraid. I couldn't pretend anymore. My mom had been involved in serious shit, whatever it was. Those two men had targeted her for a specific reason. I placed the journal back in my backpack and hung my head. Slowly, I started to breathe regularly again.

She believed in me, that I would figure this nightmare out. That mattered to me. I guess she'd left me a clue of sorts—although, right now I couldn't figure out what the hell she'd meant by it. How many puzzles had we worked on together in my lifetime? Countless. I could do this. I was smart. I was strong. I was her daughter, after all, and I would figure it out.

I raised my chin, pulled my shoulders back, and wiped my face. Slinging the pack over my shoulder, I stood to leave. In the back of the church, I stopped at the Mother Mary statue, and made the Sign of the Cross—something I'd watch my mom do many, many times in my life. In that same weird way, I sensed her with me in this place. I plunked coins into a metal box and reached for a long matchstick, striking it, and watching the flame burn its tip. I whispered a silent prayer, as I lit two votive candles—one for Mom and one for me. I figured both of us could use all the help we could get right now.

CHAPTER 14

Six Days Missing

"Feel better?" Uncle Angel asked.

He studied me, as I climbed into the passenger side. The creases and shadows around his eyes had deepened. He looked like a man haunted, and he badly needed a shave. But his glance remained as watchful as ever.

I shrugged and buckled in, avoiding his stare. There certainly was no peace inside this car. I'd left it behind in the candlelight with Mother Mary. For some unknown reason, we were still driving the rented hot rod, which grated on me. His truck remained parked inside his garage.

"That's a laugh," I said, a bitter taste springing to my mouth. "No. I won't feel better until Mom is safe at home. You get that, right?"

He was still watching me. If he had something to tell me, right now would be a good time. But he offered nothing. Except silence.

"It's gonna be okay," he finally said, a deep sigh escaping his lips, as he patted my knee. I flinched. He quickly drew his hand back.

"What the hell, Mireya? I'm trying to comfort you!"

"I'm a mess this morning, that's all." I mashed the heels of my hands against my temples. Another headache was coming. All the fucking secrets—puzzles I couldn't figure out—relentlessly tugging at parts of my brain like a taffy-pulling machine.

He muttered under his breath and maneuvered the car onto the street.

I wanted to scream at him, unload all my frustration and misery. I loved my uncle, but I didn't know who I could trust, especially since I knew in my bones he hid critical information. Why? He knew her life was at stake, and he continued to stay silent instead of sharing whatever he might know with the police. But I couldn't say anything, yet. Besides, I hadn't shared what Shilpa had told me, so maybe I wasn't any better. I forced myself to settle down, keep my temper under control. I had to stay smart if I wanted to help Mom.

"Are you working today?" I asked, trying to ease the tension inside the car.

"No," he said quietly. "I took a few weeks off. Family leave."

"Oh. Seems like you've been working a lot, like long hours. Thought you had a case."

"I do. My sister is missing," he snapped. "I'm chasing a few leads on my own, off book."

A few leads. Off book, huh? Whatever.

"Have you found anything? Any theory on who might have taken Mom? Any info the police should know about?" I asked, shooting him a pointed look.

"No, not yet," he said. "A few half-baked ideas are all, but nothing I can share, yet."

Right. Of course. Nothing he *wanted* to share was more like it.

"I want to go home. Can you take me by the house?" I knew I sounded snotty, but rage bubbled to the surface. So much for keeping my cool. I gritted my teeth. "I need more clothes, and I want my art supplies. I need to sketch or paint or something before I go insane. This endless waiting is killing me."

I heard his rough breathing, but he didn't answer me.

"I want to go home!" I repeated with force.

"No," he said, quietly. "I want you to stay away from the house for now as an extra precaution since we don't know who took her or why. Just in case it wasn't a random incident at the ATM."

"Do *you* think it wasn't random? Do the *police* think that?"

"I don't know," he said with a shrug. "These types of cases can take time."

"Are you telling me everything? Is there something else I need to know, uncle?"

"Like I told you, I'm working on it."

I pressed my lips together, balling my fists. Silence dragged out.

"Look, I know you're upset. I get it. But I forbid you to go to the house without me. Do you hear?" he asked, his voice and movements agitated.

I stared straight ahead, clenching my jaw to keep from screaming at him. When he spoke again, his tone was more relaxed. "Just a few more days, okay? I told you it's too risky to go there right now. You gotta understand."

"Why?" I shot back.

"Why what?"

"Why is it too risky to go? Explain it to me, Uncle Angel, because the police said they're finished with what they needed from our house. They took Mom's laptop, financial records—everything listed in the warrant," I said, my voice steadily increasing in volume. "I'm so tired of the cryptic-ass shit. Spit it out! Does the danger have something to do with these leads you're working 'off book'?" I asked, using the stupid air quotes he always used. "What does that even mean, anyway? Is it legal? Tell me what is going on!"

"What the hell has gotten into you?" He roared back, his anger matching mine. "I'm running my ass off here, working off the radar, trying to find her, and I don't need you screwing things up. There are things I *cannot* tell you, okay? Not right now. It's for your own damn safety—understand?"

No, I didn't. Inside, I was raging. I wanted to pin him down about the files I'd found, about what those gang members he was investigating were about, but I couldn't risk it. If he'd known I was snooping around his stuff, he'd be pissed. Plus, he'd make sure I didn't stumble onto anything else.

I needed to calm down. Staring out the window, I tried focusing on what my mom would do. She'd be smarter. She'd told me countless times, since I was a small child, that my temper got the best of me, usually when it'd work to my advantage to stay calm. Slowly, I counted to fifty under my breath.

His cell phone chimed. He dug it out of his jeans pocket as he drove, then looked at it. It continued ringing, but it wasn't coming from the phone in his hand, which he quickly shoved back into his jeans. It was coming from inside the middle console of the car.

His mouth tightened as he looked at me, then swore under his breath. He reached in and grabbed the second phone, which looked like one of those generic burner phones I'd seen used on television shows.

"I have to take this call," he said. "Listen, you have to stay quiet. Okay? Don't say a word."

"But, why do you have—"

"For god's sake, Mireya! Quiet!"

He answered the phone, speaking in a skittish cadence much different than his usual confident tone.

"Hey, man, can't talk now, the old lady's here." His voice was way low, and he'd stopped annunciating his words. It was difficult to understand. "Yeah, man, I should know more then. Yeah, yeah, that's right dude. Later."

Who had been on the other end of the line? And what was up with the second phone stashed away? He flipped the extra phone shut and tossed it into the console. He kept his eyes forward.

"Wanna tell me what that was about? Why the freaky voice? Maybe explain why you're carrying around a *burner phone*?" I shook my head in disbelief. "You look exactly like my uncle, and except for just now, you mostly sound like him. But I don't even know who you are these days."

"Listen, I can't tell you who I was talking to or why." He rubbed the side of his neck. "Like I said, not right now."

"You can't? Or you won't?" I clenched my jaw. "There's a difference, you know."

"I know the fucking difference. I *can't* tell you."

"Yeah. Right." I scowled at his profile.

"Why can't you just trust me?" He glanced my way, his voice dripping in disappointment. "Jesus, you act like I have something to do with Ana María going missing!"

I purposely raised my eyebrows at him. There, I'd done it again without thinking.

"Are you serious? This is bullshit. Talk about paranoia. Do you really think I'm capable of that—that I'd harm your mother, my own sister?" The veins in his neck popped out; it looked like his head might explode.

Mija, stop this! Inside my brain, I could hear Mom's voice reprimanding me. I shook my head vehemently no. Of course, I didn't believe he had anything to do with her disappearance. But he'd acted so strange lately, and he'd kept things from me, for sure.

"It's just, it feels like you're hiding something—something important—from me." I reached out to touch his arm, but this time he flinched. "I'm sorry. I'm not thinking straight. It's—I'm just—I'm frustrated because we haven't found her. And I'm petrified for her, you know?" It was the truth. I looked at him again, wanting to lean against him, wanting to lay my head on his shoulder and cry. But I couldn't.

"You would tell me—you'd say something to the police—if you found out anything about her disappearance, right? Like, if you had an idea who might have taken her? Or anything that might help us find her." I watched him. His face softened toward me, and he tugged on the side of his right ear.

"Of course, I'd tell you. And if I were to find any workable leads, anything that would help locate her, I'll share it right away." He placed his right hand on his chest, above his heart. "But we need to stop fighting each other—we need to remember we're family, and we both want her home. You understand we're on the same team, right? I'll do everything in my power to find her."

I stared at his chest, flicking my gaze upward toward his. My heart hammered inside my head, but my voice remained steady as I spoke. "I know. It's just—I'm freaked out by everything lately. I miss her so much, I can hardly breathe most of the time."

"I get it—I do. I miss her, too, mija. But I'm trying to keep you safe from things—things I can't go into just yet—but I can't do that, if you don't trust me."

His voice was as sweet and pure as raw honey, the deep golden kind Mom would sometimes smear on tortillas for breakfast. And I probably would have believed each word he'd said if it weren't for one thing: He was lying to me. How did I know? It was his tell, a sign that gave him away, one my mom had pointed out to me once during one of our family poker nights a couple years ago.

"Angel tugs at that right ear when he's bluffing his hand. Don't tell him I told you," she had whispered in a soft, singsong tone. "If you want to beat him, just watch. You'll see what I mean. He does it every single time."

Why was he hiding things from me? Was it to protect me? The same reason my mom had kept things from me? I didn't want his protection or, for that matter, hers either. Mom was the one who needed it. If she was mixed up with the likes of the guys in those files, we needed to find her before they did something horrible to her. Before it was too late.

"We're good, right?" Uncle Angel's question brought me back to our drive.

"Oh, yeah, we're good." I gently pulled the backpack on the floorboard closer, secure with the knowledge that mom's journal was tucked inside, then reached up to flip open the visor mirror. He watched as I rubbed at smeared mascara stains on my cheeks. As I looked into the brightness of my own eyes in my reflection, I hoped he couldn't see what I was thinking. I had a plan, a way to possibly find some workable leads of my own.

My uncle was not being truthful. He was hiding something important from me, for whatever reasons. I had to figure out why, which meant going back to our house and looking for whatever Mom might have left for me there. That's what her journal entry was about. I had always been her hope, and right now, I might be her only chance. She was leading me back home—to the place where I expected to find at least a strand of the truth. And maybe that one thread could lead me to her.

CHAPTER 15

A Week Missing

T he house was dark. Cici had dropped me off a few blocks away, where she'd wait for me. I jogged there, keeping close to houses, fences, trees, anything that provided shadow. Uncle Angel had forbidden me to go anywhere near my house.

He'd used the actual word "forbidden" twice: yesterday in the car, and last night when he caught me pulling my house keys out of the kitchen drawer where he'd stashed them. I was busted, so I explained in a stammer that I might be able to find something at the house that would help us understand what had happened to her. He had grabbed the keys from me and tucked them in his pocket.

I stomped away, but he had followed me to the guest room.

"This is *serious shit*. Your mom was forcibly taken—and I don't have the time for your Nancy Drew bullshit," he had yelled, one hand on the door jamb, his body an obstacle as much as his tone. Underneath the bluster, I heard something tinny and high-pitched. *Fear*. "You can't risk it. What if someone is watching the house? Did you think of that? What if someone tries to hurt you? I can't let that happen."

"Why?"

"Why what?"

"Why would someone be watching our house? Wasn't Mom randomly abducted at that ATM? Or is there something else you'd like to share? Do you know who took her?"

"Here we go again," he said, throwing his arms in the air. His brows were drawn together like curtains pulled tight. "Stay away from the house. What part of that can't you understand? Like I said, I forbid you to go over there until we know what's going on."

Our eyes met, each of us refusing to blink first. Then he ran his hands through his hair, swearing under his breath. He looked on the verge of exhaustion.

"Grow up, Mireya. For all our sakes," he said quietly, then walked away. I threw myself on the bed, pulling a blanket tight around my shoulders.

About ten minutes later, I heard him on the phone in the other room, speaking in that low, strange voice. Not too long after, he called out that he'd be back soon and that I should lock up while he was gone.

Whatever. The mere idea of him looming over me sparked anger deep within me. Where did he get off? Did he not want me to find something? Was that it? Was he afraid I'd stumble onto more secrets he didn't want me to know? Or was he like the rest of them, the other law enforcement officers—the Texas Rangers, the FBI, the sheriff's department, and city police—none of them telling me squat about the case. They spent a lot of time talking in hushed circles, but that's about it. I was sick of being kept in the dark about my own mother.

Fuck it. Uncle Angel could take my house keys, but he wouldn't stop me. After he'd left last night, I immediately called Cici, and we made plans for tonight. Regardless of what he'd said, I was going home to look for any signs Mom might have left me. No one knew her like I did. Maybe there were potential clues the police had missed inside our house.

It was possible. If there were something, any promising lead on where she might be, I needed to find it, even if it meant breaking into my own home against my uncle's wishes.

Cloaked by the shadow of an enormous oak tree and dressed in all-black jeans and a t-shirt, I stood in darkness across the street from our house. Several minutes ticked by. My brain filtered the familiar noises around me—two dogs yapping in the backyard a couple of houses down, the *ting-a-ling-a-ting* of chimes hanging from a tree across the street, the intermittent rumblings of crickets coming from everywhere. Then the aroma of fried onions and potatoes spiced with curry and cumin thumped my senses, the pungent smell bringing forth an image of my mother and Shilpa at work in our kitchen last year as they made samosas, my mom's favorite Indian dish.

"The potatoes are burning. You must use more oil," Shilpa had chided in a sing-song voice. I heard them laughing, as Shilpa had set about playfully barking more orders at Mom.

I blinked back tears, wishing I could reclaim that moment, have Mom standing in front of our stove, frying potatoes, a smile playing at her lips as she listened to her bossy friend. My stomach grumbled loudly, and I ducked low.

Settle down, mija, I could hear my mom say, something she'd often whisper to me when I'd get too jumpy.

I couldn't settle down, though. My senses were hyper-alert—I didn't see anything unusual, but something felt off in the air that surrounded me, as if static electricity sparked every time I moved. I quickly scanned the area again but couldn't shake the feeling someone was nearby. Watching.

I rubbed my eyes. God. My uncle was right. I was getting paranoid, probably from the constant stress. That's what Mom would say, anyway.

I had taken enough precautions to get here, though. I knew that, so I waited a few minutes more, checked and rechecked around me, then sprinted across the street and into the shadows of our house.

"You forbid me, huh, Uncle Angel?" I whispered to no one. "Well, fuck that."

Unfortunately, we didn't have a spare key hidden outside the house like most people. My crime-prevention-obsessed mom would not allow it. I pulled on leather gloves as I circled around to the backyard, then picked up a hefty rock from the garden, and tapped it against the glass pane of the back door, as quietly as I could until it broke. I looked around again to make sure I was alone, then reached inside and unlocked the door. I quickly went in, glass crunching underfoot, as I closed it behind me.

The kitchen smelled stale, unused. I quickly headed for Mom's bedroom, where once I entered, I almost crumpled to the ground. It was the scent of her, the smell of baby powder and vanilla with a touch of cinnamon. That's what hit me. The visceral pain of her absence—all the while her perfume clinging to this room—smacked me in the face like an aluminum baseball bat between the eyes. I doubled over and stifled a cry.

"Get your shit together," I muttered to myself in between gasp-sobs. My instincts were to crawl under the covers of her bed, make them like a cocoon, breathing her in all around me. But I didn't have time for that or for crying. I had to get in and get out before anyone realized I was there. My jaws clamped together so hard, my face ached. I tried to gather myself, focus my mind on the task. Like we trained our brains to do in taekwondo class. Center the energy on a focal point. Finally, I cleared my head and took out the flashlight I had shoved in my backpack earlier, moving deeper into the room.

It was Hide-and-Seek time. She had mentioned that game, specifically, so I knew she'd hidden something for me. But what was it? And where would she hide stuff, she wanted only me to find? It could be anywhere.

I started with her dresser drawers, digging through underwear and pajamas, looking for any taped envelopes underneath or behind. I checked the closet, patted down hanging clothes and went through pockets, tapped on walls, rummaged through jewelry, shimmied under the bed, the flashlight bouncing about the bedroom walls like the reflected lights of a disco ball. Nothing. Nothing in the bathroom cabinets either.

Nothing under the worn sofa cushions in the living room or in the backs of the closets, the beam of the flashlight landing on loose change and occasional floating dust bunnies. Nothing behind framed art—mostly pictures I had painted for her throughout the years—or under the furniture. Or behind her collection of elephant figurines in the living room bookcase. I proceeded through the house to my bedroom but saw no signs of anything important. I found two shirts and a pair of jeans I wanted and shoved them in my backpack, then headed for her office down the hall.

This room looked the most disturbed by police investigators. Her computer was gone, and manila files were splayed on top of her usually immaculate desktop. I ran my hands under the desk and dug through the top drawer and filing cabinet. I put my memory to work, careful to take everything in. I took books out of the small bookcase and rifled through them, stopping occasionally on dog-eared pages that had penciled notes on the sides. I ran my fingers over her handwriting and willed myself to shake off the sadness. The book collection comprised mostly poetry and fiction, many about women's issues and girl power stuff. I thought I might find something in one of them, but no. Nada. It felt strange going through her things, especially since I didn't really know what I was looking for. She hadn't given me much to go on in the journal entry.

"Mom, you have to help me," I said, my voice hushed as I continued scanning anything and everything. "Did you leave something for me? Where is it?" My hope was slipping. Maybe this was a dumb idea. A desperate grasp at thin air. "C'mon, Mom. Anything—please."

After checking every possible hiding-place I could think of, I found myself back in the kitchen. Defeat pulled down my shoulders. I doubted she'd leave anything in this room, but I still had to check. I opened the pantry door, moving cans of vegetables and boxes of cereal and rice, shaking and replacing them. I found an empty oatmeal canister with cash in it, containing mostly wadded up ones and fives. Huh. She'd never told me she kept this on hand. So many secrets, it seemed. I pocketed the cash, and as I replaced the canister in the pantry, I accidentally banged the flashlight against the shelf. It loudly ricocheted onto the floor, spinning on the tile before coming to a stop under the kitchen island.

"Damn." I squatted down to grab it. That's when I noticed the baseboard under the island. It looked slightly different. The light shone directly on it, and since I was almost nose-to-nose with it, I could see two vertical hairline fractures, parallel along the baseboard, about ten inches apart. *Strange.* Studying it, I pushed on the baseboard, but it didn't move. I tapped on it and heard a hollow sound. A spiking sensation of adrenaline coursed through me. *Maybe. Just maybe.* I grabbed the Swiss Army knife from my backpack, whacking it a few times to loosen it if I could, and then prodded under the crease of the baseboard, where it met the floor. A segment of the board popped out. Surprised, I peered inside the gaping hole that had been hidden behind it.

"Bingo," I said to myself. It made sense now. She had written in her journal about how I had to touch base before I could win, and the kitchen island was the perfect place for home base in a game of Hide-and-Seek. When I was little, we played it together, and no matter where we lived, the kitchen was always home. Why hadn't I thought of that, initially?

I would have never found the stash if it hadn't been for the dropped flashlight. I couldn't help but wonder if Mom was there with me, nudging me in the right direction so I could find her.

Carefully, I pulled out small bundles of rolled-up cash, all one-hundred-dollar bills, along with several newspaper clippings and a small pistol. *WTF?* The chill of the metal against my fingertips caused me to shiver. I had never touched a gun before. My mother hated guns. And then there were the passports I had never seen before: Four had photos of Mom, another had a recent picture of me, and the last a photo of Uncle Angel. But each had a different name—the wrong names—on them. They looked legit, but they had to be fake passports, the likes of which I'd only seen in movies. Where would she get these and why did she want them?

I pressed my lips together so hard, it hurt, and gulped at the acid rising in my throat. "What have you been up to, Mom?"

Before I could process, I heard a *thunk* at the front door. Then another *thunk*. Someone was trying to get into the house. Had Uncle Angel been right? Was there someone watching our house? I had to get the hell out of there.

"Oh, shit. Oh, shit." Gathering the money, the newspaper articles, the gun, and passports, I frantically shoved them in the backpack and quietly replaced the baseboard to hide the gap. I had no idea who was out there. Another *thunk*, this one the loudest and sharpest of all.

Swallowing a scream, I scrambled to my feet and bolted for the back door, just as I heard someone crash through the front. I closed it behind me as gently as I could with fumbling hands and shot into the shadows, headed in the direction of Cici's car, using the back alleys this time. Constantly looking around me, I stuck to the darkness, my insides shaking, my heart pounding too loud in my ears. Beads of sweat covered my upper lip when I finally came out on the street and neared the parked car about two blocks from our house. I waited near a tall shrub, scouting the area around me, and spotted a man on foot flitting in and out of parked cars not far from where Cici was. She must have had earbuds on, because I watched her head bobbing silently, and her hands drumming a rhythm on the steering wheel. I tried texting her a warning, but no response.

"Cici, look up. Look up!" I whispered to her, wishing she could hear me. I couldn't believe it. Multiple thoughts zoomed inside my head. The man was headed right toward her car. He'd see her in a few seconds. What if he mistakes Cici for me? Would he hurt her? It had to be the same person who broke down the door. Why else would this man be skulking in the dark like that? Who was he and why had he broken into my house? Had he taken my mom at the ATM? Was the other guy around here, too? I checked the surrounding area again but didn't see anyone else.

"Okay—okay," I mumbled to myself. "Think."

My entire body shook with fear as I blindly grabbed for the gun inside my backpack. It was small and cold in my burning palm, slick with sweat. He was close enough that I could hear his steady steps moving toward Cici's car. He stopped here and there, looking behind and under parked automobiles. At this point, there was only one thing I could do. Make it to the car and get the hell out of here.

Focus.

I held the weight of the gun in both hands, not having any idea of how to use it or if it had a safety or whatever. But I figured I could always point it and find out. If this man was responsible for my mom's disappearance, I could pull the trigger. But I didn't know. After seeing all that money and fake passports, I wasn't sure about anything anymore. What if it was actually a cop who saw my flashlight in the house? Or maybe a neighborhood security guy?

The man was so close now. He was almost to the car, and Cici sat there, oblivious. I had to take the chance. With unstable hands, I zeroed in on him. Then I shifted my gaze a few feet behind him, raised one arm, and threw the pistol as hard as I could, watching it cartwheel high above in an arc before crashing against the window of a nearby parked car. A shot went off, and the car alarm *bleeped-bleeped-bleeped* as the man spun around and ducked. It must have fired when it hit the vehicle. I didn't mean for it to go off, but I knew nothing about guns. Hunched low to the ground, he slowly moved away from Cici. Porch lights along the street came on almost instantly, as the car alarm continued squawking.

I tiptoed in the shadow of the shrubs as quiet as I could, then made a frantic sprint for the car, never running as fast as that moment. I made it to the passengers' side, diving in and slamming the door.

"Did you hear that? It sounded like gunsho—" Cici squeaked, craning her neck around.

"Go! Go! Go!" I roared, watching in the side mirror, as the car rumbled to life and his head swiveled toward the sound. Our eyes met briefly, then he rocketed forward.

"GO!"

Cici punched the gas to the floorboard, the tires squealing out onto the street just as he neared. The smell of burned rubber surrounded me. In the mirror, I saw him raise both arms and fire, then the side mirror shattered into tiny pieces.

Both Cici and I screamed, as we raced away, running stop signs, praying she didn't hit anyone, but too scared to stop. Before he had shot at me, I had seen his face. He looked vaguely familiar, like someone I should know, but I couldn't place him. Was it a friend of my mom's I had met before? Someone at school or church. Could it be one of the guys in my uncle's files?

I clutched the grab handle of the car door, my knuckles turning white, as we drove back to Uncle Angel's house. I pressed the backpack to my chest with the other arm, my mind replaying what had just gone down. I couldn't manage any words, and Cici didn't say anything either. That was no cop back there. That man had fired a gun at me, and if he had shot at me, he'd shoot at my mother, too. That's if he hadn't already. It made me nauseous to even consider the possibility.

Uncle Angel wasn't home when Cici pulled into the driveway. At least that was a good thing. He'd never know I'd gone against his wishes. It'd give me time to get my rattled nerves under control.

Cici turned off the ignition. She slumped against the steering wheel, so I reached over and hugged her. We were both still in shock.

"What. The. Actual. Fuck," Cici said in a shaky voice. "I can't believe—"

"I'm so sorry. I didn't know," I said, softly, sitting back, and eyeing the shattered side mirror. "I had no idea that would happen. I would never put you in that kind of danger. I can't even process what just happened."

"I've never been so scared in my life," she said, her skinny arms wrapped around her torso. "What do we do now? Call the police?"

"No, not yet. Let me talk to my uncle first."

Her forehead scrunched as she looked at me.

"But someone shot at us, Mireya. With a real gun! We could have been killed." She shivered, motioning to the damaged mirror. "How am I supposed to explain that to my parents?"

Cici's phone rang before I could respond. She shushed me before she answered.

"Hey, Mom. Yeah, we're at Angel's right now going over some of the schoolwork Mireya has missed. Uhhhmmm. Yeah, I'm getting ready to leave now," she said in an ultra-calm voice. "Hey, do you think you or dad could wait for me in the driveway? Someone must have sideswiped my car on the street." She paused. "Looks like they took out the side mirror. That's it. Yeah, yeah. I'll show you as soon as I get home."

I was afraid to get out of her car, go into an empty darkened house. When I gave her the all-clear, she took off. A part of me wanted her to wait until my uncle got home. But the other half of my brain began to fill with rage, a red veil dipping into my vision. I understood now. I was being hunted—just as my mother had been. And if I had fully comprehended that earlier, I would have played that last scenario with the man much differently. Instead of running or throwing a gun to distract him, I would have stood my ground—I would have shot the monster dead.

CHAPTER 16

A Week Missing

I was ready for Uncle Angel when he came home. I'd had enough of his lies, and I told him so, letting him know what had happened to Cici and me a few hours earlier. He turned pale as I recounted how the man had broken into my house and had later shot at us as we escaped in the car.

"What the hell do you think you're playing at, Mireya? I told you not to go back there! I explicitly said it could be dangerous! Then you drag your friend into it? Nearly get the both of you killed?" Uncle Angel shouted as he paced in front of me, pulling the hair at his temples. He was unraveling before me. In my entire seventeen years, I'd never seen the man cry, but it looked possible now. He groaned, then whimpered. "We are so screwed—you have no idea."

"No, I don't. Why don't you fill me in?" I watched him, my face blank of the fear I felt bubbling in my stomach, but also devoid of the rage that stiffened my neck and shoulders, holding me erect in the chair. I channeled my mother, how she would confront her brother if she were in this situation. She'd be fierce.

"Listen, you're not telling me everything you know," I said in an icy voice, motioning to the items I'd recovered at our house that were now spread across his kitchen table. "I read the articles. Found what looks like Mom's go-box?"

"Her what?" He stopped in front of me. "How do you know about go-boxes?"

"Because I like spy movies. Who knew I'd ever actually see this shit in real life." I paused, scowling hard at him. "Enough. You need to tell me what the hell's going on, Uncle. I mean it."

He scoffed at the items, then moved to the door to check the deadbolt, and next to the windows to tighten the blinds. Uncle Angel's skin looked clammy, like he might possibly stroke out on me. But I was too livid to care. He wouldn't meet my eyes as he sat down on the edge of the chair.

"Where did Mom get all this money?" I asked, pointing to the carefully wrapped green bundles stacked on the table. There was at least $50,000 in cash, easy. Was it even real money or could it be counterfeit, like the bogus passports for all three of us? I had never seen so much money.

I grabbed one of the passports and tossed it toward him with the cover open. It thumped on the tabletop in front of him.

"Nice photo, right?" He looked down at the image of himself staring back and swallowed. "Did *you* know about this? Maybe you helped Mom hide this in our house. Like I said, you know more than you're letting on. That much I've figured out."

I brushed my fingertips over the newspaper clippings yellowed with age. The news stories covered the trials of three coyotes who oversaw a sex trafficking operation on the Mexico-New Mexico border back in 2006. Another article had a sketch of a fourth man, his eyes hidden by aviator sunglasses, allegedly the mastermind who had escaped during a huge raid on one of the sex camps. He was still on the run when the trials occurred and had never been found.

"So, tell me about these guys." I slid the newsprint toward him, tapping it with my fingernail. He glanced at it, a light flush slowly making its way up his neck and face. At least he finally had color in his face. "I'm guessing you know something about it. You were a border agent about that time, right? Were you involved in the raid? Were you a part of this trial?"

Silence. He looked away, as he clawed the stubble on both sides of his face, his eyes darting around the room. Finally, he focused on my face.

"We can't be sure you weren't followed here. We have to leave." He had a touch of crazy in his look. But I didn't care. I felt a tad insane myself.

"I'm not going anywhere. Not until I know what's going on." I gestured at the items in front of me. "Like I said, you've been lying to me. Don't even try to deny it." I crossed my arms and worked my jaw to contain my anger. "Is this your fault? Was my mom—*your sister*—abducted at gunpoint because of something *you* did? Are you a dirty cop? Maybe that's what's behind this nightmare?"

He ignored me. "Pack a bag, míja. We need to leave. Get somewhere secure." He moved into action, striding down the hall toward his bedroom, calling over his shoulder, "Do it! Now!"

"Wait a minute. I'm not done!" I walked to his room, and immediately heard the stuttering sound of heavy furniture moving against the wood floor, then a loud knocking. "What the hell are you—" I said as I entered the door and found my uncle pulling more stacks of cash from an uncovered hole at the baseboard behind his bed. He shoved them in a gym bag. "My God. Where did you—" I couldn't finish my questions. I clung to the door frame, open-mouthed. He was a DEA agent, a law enforcement officer, and I find him digging through a secret hiding place where he stashed wads of cash, just like Mom.

He looked up. "Get your shit packed," he barked. "Move. Your. Ass." For the first time ever, he frightened me. His eyes had turned stony now, the eyes of a stranger, not of my uncle.

I backed away. My brain couldn't process all that was happening, what had already happened. The past few weeks—Mom's abduction, the police questioning me, the grim searches for bodies in pastures, the mysterious cash, all the secrets, the feeling in my gut she was dead, that bullet—the one meant for me—shattering the car mirror, my uncle's constant lies. I wanted our boring life back. Not any of this. But even more than that, I wanted my mom back. That, and the truth. I deserved to have them both.

That was it. Enough of his bullshit. Neither of us were going anywhere until he told me everything that he knew. I sprinted down the hall to the pile on the table, and in one motion, swept it into my backpack, cash and all. I shouldered it, then walked to the gun cabinet in the living room where Uncle Angel kept a loaded shotgun. He had given me the combination, my birthdate, a few days earlier. I grabbed it out of the case and thumbed the safety off, the way he had showed me. Although I'd never fired it, or even touched it, I had a decent idea how to hold it. It was heavy and unyielding in my hands, but I gripped it tight, the butt of it nestled in my armpit. My uncle continued making noises as he packed in his room.

"You ready?" he called down the hall, headed my way. "Okay, so we can take the car, then we'll ditch it along—" He stopped abruptly as he registered the shotgun barrel pointed in his direction. His brow crinkled in irritation. "Whoa, Mireya. You know better than to point that thing at me. Too dangerous. The safety should be on—but still. Put it down."

Still talking, he moved to the counter to grab his wallet. "Glad you thought of taking the shotgun, though. Good idea. You don't even have to aim to hit your target with that one."

"I'm not going," I said, my voice dull. That's how I felt, flat and dead, a buzzing like flies filling my head.

"The fuck, Mireya." He turned to face me, shaking his head. He voice was equally quiet and flat. "We don't have time for fucking teen drama."

"Sit down. Take the pistol out of your holster and slowly put it on the floor." It was a sentence I never thought I'd have to utter in my life. And certainly not to Uncle Angel, the man who helped raise me and was the only father figure I'd ever known.

"Are you serious? Stop the bullshit," he said. "We seriously don't have time for this. You're not straight in the head. I get it. Too much—"

"Do it!" I shouted, squinting at him. A part of my brain registered how crazy I was behaving, but under the circumstances, I cut myself some slack.

"You would *shoot me*? I don't think you would." But maybe something in my eyes told him not to risk it. He shook his head, a deep disappointment in the dip of his chin, but he slowly placed the gun on the ground.

"Now sit down at the table and spill it all," I said, waving the shotgun barrel in that direction. "And I mean *all* of it."

"This—" he waved toward the backpack I carried, "this is not what you think. I can explain on the road, but let's get going before it's too late. We need to find a safe—"

"Shut up!" I roared, then added more softly, "The longer you drag this out, the longer it'll take us to leave. I'm not going anywhere until you tell me what you and Mom have been up to."

He stood frozen before me. I sensed an internal debate raging within him from the looks that flashed across his face. It ran the gambit—fear, fury, indignation, concern. Again, none of it mattered to me. I was past caring about anything but the truth. In the end, he groaned in resignation.

"I'm sorry." His palms faced me as he sat down at the chair. "I never meant for any of this to happen. Neither did your mom." The moodiness in Uncle Angel's face changed again. His eyes began to water. "I'm not sure where to start."

"How about the beginning."

"The beginning. Right. Okay." He leaned forward and buried his head in his hands. "This is difficult to say. First thing is—and I don't even know how to tell you this—but I'm not who you think I am. I'm not—" He coughed and swiped at his eyes. "The thing is—I'm not really your uncle. Not in the biological sense, anyway, but I love you like you're my own. You know that."

Many things had run through my mind, but I would have never predicted this revelation. Never in a million possible scenarios. My mouth hung open.

Words began filling the room. It was like he couldn't stop talking once he began, like he needed to unload what he'd been carrying around. He had been a border agent, headed home one early morning after a late shift, driving in the middle of nowhere on the New Mexico border, when his headlights illuminated what looked like a large mound of dirt on the side of the road. He realized, as he saw the mound move, that it was not what he'd initially thought. Not even close.

"It turned out to be a young woman, caked in grime, clutching this dirty bundle of rags. But it wasn't just rags, mija," he said with emotion. "It was your mom—holding you."

"What?" I managed to get out. "I'm not following. Me and mom? How is that even possible? Why was she out there?"

"Please, let me finish, then you can ask questions, okay? I know this is a lot, but I need to explain. She was young, about your age, covered in dirt and ant bites and scratches from head-to-toe. At first, she tried to run from me. I could tell she was petrified when she saw me get out of the truck, even though I tried reassuring her that I wouldn't hurt her, but she didn't have enough strength to get too far or to fight me, like she tried to do." He ran fingers through his hair. "Apparently, she'd been walking for days, she wasn't even aware of how many. It had been below freezing at night, and hot as hell during the days. I'm not sure how either of you survived."

"I remember, she had this backpack filled with stuff, but she said she'd run out of water the second day." He leaned back in the chair and tapped his fingertips on the tabletop, lost in thought. He finally spoke again.

"Here's the reality—and it's not pretty. I broke the law that night, and several more times after that, when I arranged fake identities for the both of you. As soon as I saw you, I should have turned you both over to the border authorities, but something about your mom, how defiant she was even though she couldn't have been more vulnerable out there in the middle of nowhere, reminded me of my own mom. She'd been a fighter, too. I had to help Ana María. I couldn't put you two into the system—especially after she told me the truth about you."

"The truth?" I asked, my voice raspy, the shotgun now dangling in front of me, pointed at my feet. My throat tightened as I held back tears, making it painful to swallow, like I had a chunk of hard candy lodged at the back. My mind clicked into another mode, like I was floating above, watching the conversation take place below me. Nothing he said seemed real. Just a man retelling a distant dream.

He blinked rapidly before slumping forward. All his frantic energy from a few minutes ago zapped. "It's not really my story to tell." He bowed his head, staring at the table. "It's your mom's story. She should be the one telling you what happened—how she wound up there with you."

"But it's *my* story, too," I said, "and I have the right to hear it. Especially if it has anything to do with what has happened to her."

He raised his head, a pained expression set in the lines of his face.

"I don't even know how to tell you this, but I'll try. Your mom—" he said, before clearing his throat.

"She was one of the girls taken for that trafficking ring you read about," he continued, his voice coming out almost in a whisper now, gesturing to the backpack that contained the articles. "You're certain you want to hear this? The no-bullshit version."

"Yes," I said, as my gut tightened, preparing for the blows to come. "No more bullshit. We need to find her, and maybe this will help."

He nodded at me. I'd never seen him look so dejected.

"She and her sister—they were only fifteen and thirteen-years-old when they were abducted from Albuquerque and taken to one of the tent camps that was used to house the girls near the border. Workers would, uh, visit the camps—for drugs and women. They were imprisoned for almost two years by those fucking animals—the men you read about in the news clippings."

I was no longer floating above in my mind. His words brought me crashing to the ground, back to a reality, where everything became sharp and blinding and painful. A roiling began in the pit of my stomach. My mother had been brutally forced into sex trafficking. That's what he couldn't manage to say. Those were the words he kept biting back.

"And what happened to the younger sister? Where is she now?" My voice was hushed, like we were in the middle of Mass. A dread settled in my chest.

Uncle Angel coughed, steepled his fingers in front of him and closed his eyes. Sweat dotted his upper lip. He struggled to get the words out. "She—I never met her, but your mom said—her sister died at the camp minutes before a surprise raid by Mexican federales and U.S. authorities. Ana María panicked, had no idea what was happening or who was raiding the camp, so she fled with you in her arms. She somehow managed to escape in the chaos."

"Oh," I managed in a strangled voice. So much began to make sense. My mother's night terrors ever since I could remember. Her overly protective ways. Her hypervigilance—how she constantly looked for potential threats in most everyone we met. Her determination that I learn how to defend myself with martial arts.

"It's horrible, what happened to her—except for you, Mireya. She never regretted you." But there was something else he was struggling to say. I could see it as he looked at me, his mouth moving every so often, but no words coming out. It looked like he had rapidly aged in the past twenty minutes.

"There's one more thing," he said, his voice breaking. He entwined his fingers in front of his mouth. It was obvious he dreaded telling me.

"What is it?" I propped the shotgun against the table, suddenly breathless. My instinct guided me to sit down for whatever he was about to say. Maybe he was mirroring me, but Uncle Angel looked like he might throw up.

"Your mom's sister, the one who died—Mireya, there's no easy way to tell you this—she was, um—*she* was your biological mom," he choked out. His words lost their sharpness, like he suddenly spoke from underwater. Muted and garbled and slow motion. I tried to shake off the spinning sensation inside my head, the fuzzy edges that blurred my peripheral vision, but it felt like I was riding a tilt-a-whirl. "I'm sorry, mija, but your biological mom—she died while giving birth to you just before the place was raided."

"Dear god," I managed to get out. My tongue stuck to the roof of my suddenly dry mouth. So many questions sprang to mind, but I had no way to articulate them at that moment. Not in a way that made sense, anyway.

"The woman you've always known as your mom—" He pressed a knuckle to his forehead. He seemed to be in agony, but he bit the words out. "Ana María is actually your aunt. But she has loved you like you were her own. I have never seen a mother love a daughter as much as she loves you."

My aunt, my mom. I let it roll over my body like warm waves lapping against me in the Gulf of Mexico. The ugliness of lives created and altered by lies and secrets and force. All the family stories I hadn't heard growing up, the lack of extended family excused away by dead parents, the absence of a father explained as a brief but violent affair best left in the past. My mom probably had no idea who my father was. It could have been any one of the men who spent time with her sister when they "visited" the camp.

My poor mother who birthed me, who died having me at fifteen years old, according to my rough estimation. The aunt who raised me like her own when she was only seventeen. I couldn't imagine being my age and becoming a mother, much less taking care of someone else's child. The self-sacrifice was admirable, but I didn't know how she had done it. My birth had changed her life and chained her to a past I'm sure she'd have rather forgotten. I sucked in a deep breath, and a profound sadness filled my lungs, my soul, settling in for a long stay. I owed her so much.

I gathered resolve and asked Uncle Angel a few more questions. "Do you think the reason those men took her is connected to the past? To that camp? And why would they wait until now? Why didn't they track her down years ago?"

I shrunk from the fear on his face.

"I'm not sure. I've been trying to find out." His nostrils flared as he met my eyes. "But that fourth coyote you probably read about in the articles. The one in the sketch? He has been hidden, supposedly working underground for years. But I think he's resurfaced, and he's extremely dangerous. I believe he's the one who took Ana María."

That's the reason my uncle had been so secretive about what he was up to. Those men in the files must be connected to the fourth coyote. The reality of what all this could mean for my mom settled heavier on my shoulders.

"Is there a chance she's still alive?" I asked, barely able to get the words out.

"I don't know," he said. "I haven't been able to pin down anything or anyone, yet, but I'm working on it. I've been reaching out to various sources, informants I've used in past cases. That's why I've kept this all secret. I've broken the rules on so many levels, but I'm using whatever resource I have access to, doing whatever I can to help find your mom. I'll face the repercussions later."

"I understand," I said, lifting my chin a fraction higher. An eerie calmness had settled over me. "What can I do? I want to help."

"First thing—let's get the hell out of here, in case you were followed," he said, getting up from the chair, but stopping to pull me up into a tight hug. "I'm sorry I kept information from you. I wanted your mom to be the one to tell you everything."

I nodded my head. If I had known this earlier, I might have had a chance to stop at least one of her abductors. For the second time that night, the thought came to me. A cold truth in the center of my being. I could do it. I could kill someone—anyone who threatened to hurt my mother—if it meant saving her life.

CHAPTER 17

Eight Days Missing

T he next morning it rained, as we drove northeast toward Spotted Fawn Lake, a body of water more like a large pond, surrounded by a handful of cozy cabins nestled among the towering pines of East Texas. Uncle Angel had bought a place there a few years back as a secluded get-away for us, though at the time I hadn't known he'd purchased it under an alias, a detail he revealed as we made our way in the rain. We all enjoyed going to the lake, but no one more than my mom. The peacefulness of the Pineywoods lured her as often as she could get away, whether we had unbearably high temps in the summer or dreary cold days in the dead of winter.

We'd taken off from the house while it was still dark outside. Once he was certain we weren't being followed—which required countless turns, doubling-back and zig-zag routes—he headed to a storage facility in a neighboring city, where he had another car waiting. This one was a plain, gray four-door sedan. I didn't react when he backed it out and pulled his pickup truck inside the storage garage. We'd left his rented hot rod parked in the driveway and set a time for the lights inside the house to turn on and off, making it look like someone was home.

The cloak-and-dagger stuff made more sense to me now. We'd stayed awake all night discussing what had happened to Mom before I was born, and the clandestine life we had all led after. He and Mom had made sure to keep fake passports up-to-date in case the truth of what they had done had ever gotten out. Uncle Angel had squirreled away cash over the years to have on hand, if we ever needed to flee the country. And, although it didn't explain my mom's large stash of money, at least I had a logical explanation for the phony IDs in the hidden duffle bag. It also made clear why we had moved so often, a sore spot for me as a child trying to plant roots. But now I understood it had been for our safety. If my uncle's theory was correct, my mom had been taken by a monster—once when she was a teen and again as a woman—a man who had killed countless people to protect a well-hidden trafficking operation along the border.

The worst part was she had never identified the mystery man, known only as the fourth coyote, nor had his colleagues, who all apparently died in various prison altercations. Two had died as inmates at different facilities by stabbings with toothbrushes-turned-shivs, their assailants unknown. The other had been smothered while sleeping, with guards pleading ignorance as to how the attacker was able to get into a locked-down cell. If she knew the silent fourth coyote's name or any details about him, Mom had never revealed them to my uncle. She'd exposed specific details about the trafficking ring, enough to shut it down, but nothing else, he said. Who knows. Maybe she had been too frightened to utter the fourth guy's name. Or maybe she didn't know it to begin with.

"We'll be there in a few hours," Uncle Angel said, nudging my leg. Powdered sugar dusted his stubbly chin, a remnant of the pack of mini doughnuts he'd devoured after we stopped at a gas station on the interstate. His haggard face folded into a grin. "Maybe you should try for some sleep, huh? You're looking rough these days."

I returned the tired smile. "Like you?"

"Yeah, something like that."

The wipers swished hypnotically, as raindrops tapped the windshield and tires hummed below. Classic country music played quietly on the stereo. A fiddle softly crying, accompanied by a baritone's brokenhearted twang. My eyelids drooped. Maybe I could close them for a few minutes.

"Sure you're good to drive?" I asked, trying to hide a yawn.

"Of course." He slurped coffee out of a jumbo Styrofoam cup. "Rest. I got this."

I eased back in the seat and threw an arm over my face. I was out within seconds.

***

I dreamed we rode in a dirt-covered RV, or maybe we were in the cab of a semi-truck, I couldn't really tell. But we were barreling down a narrow highway, surrounded by desert. At first, my mom was laughing, her hands lightly gripping the massive steering wheel as she drove. She looked like Mom but younger, more carefree than I remembered. The dimple in her cheek deepened as she turned playfully toward me.

An instant later, a streak in front of us caught my eye.

"Mom," I screamed. "You're about to hit—"

"Have faith, Mireya," she snorted, wind tussling her hair, backlit by a glaring light. Then shadows closed in.

Next thing I knew we were snuggled by a campfire, its flames almost blinding. A heavy darkness lay just outside the ring of light, and a terror clawed from within my belly. I couldn't grasp the reason for my fear. I wrapped my arms tighter around her waist.

"Something's wrong," I whispered against her chest, hearing the steady drum of her heart. The side of my cheek pressed hard into the silver elephant pendant that always dangled around her neck. I tried to push it away, but it dug deeper into my flesh. "Did you hear me? Something's wrong!"

She didn't respond but squeezed tighter.

"I'm afraid," I whimpered. Still no answer. "I'm scared—"

"I'm not afraid," she said, suddenly, sounding almost manic. She smiled against my hair and inhaled. "Wanna know why?"

"Why? Aren't you scared?" My heart tapped frantically against my own chest. My lungs ached, as I tried to breathe. An evil presence—I could feel it, but couldn't name it—hemmed us in, waiting just outside the campfire's blaze.

The flames climbed higher and higher, now surrounding us like an expansive, jagged wall that seemed to breathe when I did. I shuddered and buried my face deeper, away from the heat. I ignored the pendant digging into the side of my face.

"I'm not afraid because you're here with me," my mom said simply, with a shrug of her shoulders. Her honeyed voice was tender, overflowing with love, but with an unfamiliar twang. "She's here with me, too, you know?"

"Who?" I shifted away to look at her, but it wasn't Mom anymore. It was a young woman who resembled me. Except for the light brown color of her irises, she looked like me when I was in seventh grade, cinnamon hair escaping a messy ponytail, the same light olive complexion. She even wore my One Direction t-shirt, my favorite band at that time.

"I don't understand," I said to myself and to the person who looked like me but wasn't.

"Me, neither. I never did, really," she said, her eyes wide as she tilted her head. Flames flickered within her enormous pupils. "I couldn't escape it, you know—but you can. Will you do that for me?"

"Couldn't escape what?" I said, a frustration tugging at me, as the darkness bore down on us, prying its fingers through the inferno, trying to snake through. But I reminded myself this wasn't real. None of it was real. I could end it anytime I wanted.

"Wake up," I told myself. "This is a nightmare. That's all."

"Maybe it is," she said, gently. "But, wait, give me a second to get a good look at you."

Her hand cupped the side of my face.

"You're lovely," she said, in a wondrous tone. I instinctively closed my eyes and leaned against the velvety sensation of her touch, a vibration humming through me as her fingers caressed my cheek. An indescribable feeling of love, primal and much deeper than I could possibly grasp, spread throughout me. It was as if magic coursed through my blood at her touch. I moved even closer as she whispered, "You are all that I dreamed of, and so much more."

"Mireya," my mother's voice boomed inside my head. I jerked my eyes open to see her before me again. Her jaw was set, and her look burned with determination. "It's okay to be frightened, my love, but you must be ready. I'll be with you when it comes, but you must be prepared."

I grasped her hand, staring at the reflections dancing within her pupils before the rising flames licked at where her mouth, her cheeks, her face had been, replaced by fluid, inky shadows.

"Mamí!" I screamed, as the void quickly swallowed her whole, leaving me in total blackness, grasping nothing. It was as if she had never been there. I bellowed into the void, a wounded animal. "Maaaaaaa-mí!"

....

"Jesus, Mireya!" Uncle Angel was shouting as he shook me. He had pulled over onto the shoulder of the highway. "Are you okay? You were having a nightmare. I couldn't get you to wake up."

I stared at him, open-mouthed, trying to process what I had seen. The terrifying images remained vivid in my mind's eye.

"You drifted off, then you started yelling, not making any sense," he said, looking shaken as he patted my hair. "Must have been intense. God, you scared the hell outta me."

I focused on the powdered sugar coating his chin, but my mind still saw the flames and then the engulfing shadows.

"Hey." He snapped fingers in front of my face. "Hey. Seriously. Talk to me. What's going on? Can you wake up for me?"

Still dazed, I finally nodded.

"Mom was—" I started, then swallowed hard. "I think Mom is trying to warn us about that fourth man. I think he's coming for us, Uncle Angel. He's coming for us, just like he did for her."

Did I believe she was speaking to me? Damn straight, I did. She'd always told me her mother had been considered a bruja, someone with sight into the spirit world, as was her grandmother. Mom wasn't weird about it, but she believed science couldn't explain all mysteries within our own world, so she went with it. She couldn't rationalize it, but she had a way of knowing things, and she'd also put a lot of stock in dreams. She'd once told me our brains picked up more information than we probably realized, so maybe they filtered that data we weren't cognizant of and used the stories in our dreams to help make sense of it. I didn't know, for sure, but my intuition told me to listen.

Maybe the dream I'd just experienced made absolutely no sense, but its overall message spoke to me. The resolve in my mother's face came into vision, and I knew she was right. As always. This time when he came, we had to be ready. Like she'd told me, *I had to be ready.* Along with my uncle's help, I'd devise a plan—a way to lure him out of the shadows to a predetermined location. If he believed my mother had shared unknown details with me about his trafficking operation, as my uncle assumed, I'd be the obvious bait. Uncle Angel could be hiding, ready to jump in when needed. But first I'd get the fourth coyote to talk, find out where he'd taken Mom, and I'd record it all. We'd have the evidence we needed to put him away. We'd stomp out the fucking monster before he could hurt anyone else.

CHAPTER 18

Nine Days Missing

U ncle Angel refused to formulate any type of plan that used me as bait. He called it a crackpot strategy.

"A teenager attempting to catch a hardened criminal capable of anything? No thanks," he said, after I'd pitched the idea over breakfast at the cabin. "Not up for discussion."

He shot down every point I made. Maybe it wasn't the best idea, but he didn't offer much either, other than making phone calls.

"But—" I said, readying for another round of debate.

"Stop, Mireya," he said, his brows furrowing, dumping unfinished cereal down the garbage disposal. "I do this for a living, remember? It's not a good idea. Trust me, if there's a way you can help me find this guy, I'll put you to work. Promise. But for now, let me do this my way—please. I'm still working contacts, trying to figure out who this mystery man is." he said.

I grudgingly agreed.

While Uncle Angel worked the phone, I practiced taekwondo for a couple of hours on the grass out back near the water. Instead of my usual white gee, my standard martial arts uniform, I wore leggings and an oversized sweatshirt, training with a makeshift kick bag—a plastic garbage sack stuffed to its seams with leaves and pine needles. It dangled from a large tree limb in front of me. I'd even taped an outline of a person on the front. It looked ridiculous, but at least it allowed me to focus on a target. It felt good to hit something, and I thoroughly enjoyed kicking the crap out of it, imagining it was one of the men who had taken my mom.

The grounds were quiet except for the occasional *kihap* I bellowed, as I focused my energy on blocking, punching, chopping, and kicking techniques. I didn't hold back from hitting it with full force. I'd done this for so much of my life that once I began, my muscles gracefully moved into a controlled dance, as I completed each form. I was in a zone when my uncle called from the back porch. I had no idea how long he'd been leaning against the wood railing, watching me.

"Impressive," he said once I finished the last form. I bowed to an imaginary opponent and faced him. "I can see why you earned black belt last year. You make it look elegant, like I'm watching a ballet or something."

"Thanks." I reached back and tied my hair in a knot. Moving through taekwondo forms gave me an outlet to express myself in a controlled, powerful way, something I needed right now in all the chaos. I felt less helpless, more focused and confident.

"You up for a sandwich? I'm ready to crack open the P&J."

"Sure." I hadn't eaten since early that morning. We'd been at the lake two days, and as far as I knew, the police still didn't have any new information on my mom's whereabouts. My uncle kept busy on the phone and digging through files. I'm not sure he'd slept much since we'd arrived.

As he went back inside, I grabbed my phone from the railing and quickly scrolled through it. I'd missed two calls from Cici and umpteen texts from her and Luka. They had apparently left school early and were on their way to the cabin. *YES!* I could use some normal conversation. Cici, who had come here many times in the past with my family, was driving.

"Will you pour me some iced tea?" I called to Uncle Angel. "By the way, Cici and Luka are on their way as we speak!"

"What? Here?" He popped his head out the screen door. "Why?"

I shrugged, still thumbing through texts I hadn't seen. "Dunno. Guess they're coming to check on me? Maybe say hi?"

I looked up at his frowning face.

"Company is not a good idea right now," he said. "Remember, you two were shot at by an unknown suspect the other night? Coming here, well, it's not exactly putting your friends in a safe situation."

That stung. My eyes started watering. I didn't want to put Cici in any more danger than I already had. I felt guilty enough as it was.

"You're probably right. What do I do? They're already on the way."

He took in my near-tears and blew out a loud sigh, shaking his head.

"Call Cici. Now. If they're headed here, I need to speak to them, make sure they know what to do so they're not followed." He had that cop voice turned on again. *So much for normal.*

Cici answered on the first ring. "Hey! You're on speaker."

"Hey. I just saw your texts. Where are you?"

"About an hour away," Luka responded in that velvety tone of his. My heartbeat spluttered in my chest, as usual. "Want us to pick up anything for you before we get there?"

"I think we're good, but my uncle wants to talk to you." My face warmed at the sound of Luka's voice, and I smiled at the phone, as I stepped inside the cabin. "Here, I'll let him explain."

I didn't want to freak them out about possibly being followed, so I let Uncle Angel break it to them. He asked them a series of questions, then instructed them on defensive maneuvers to take while driving. I heard Cici tell him she had already taken some precautions, including doubling back and staying off the interstate. She had also chosen the route that wove through several small towns, most with thirty-mile-per-hour speed traps. If they were being followed, it'd be easy to spot someone that way.

Toward the end of the conversation, Cici's voice went in and out, then the line went dead. The spotty reception in the cabin was probably at play again, but still, it made me nervous. Uncle Angel shrugged and tossed the phone back to me.

"Do you think they're okay?" I nibbled on a thumbnail. It didn't take much to make me anxious these days. What if something had happened to them because they were coming to see me? What if they had been followed? I tried to dial them back three consecutive times, but each time it went straight to voicemail.

"Don't worry. You know what cell reception is like out here. They're probably in a dead coverage area. Sounds like they did everything they could to avoid being tailed," he said. "It's all good. They'll be here soon."

He turned back toward the sandwiches, quickly slathering peanut butter and jelly on slices of wheat bread and handing one to me. Then he made two for himself and opened a bag of potato chips, sliding them toward me on the bar.

"So, before they get here, lemme fill you in on what I found out just now," he said, pouring a glass of sweet tea and passing it to me. I took a quick swig. "We may have a lead on the fourth guy."

"What's—his—name?" I choked on the tea, stuttering between coughing and breathing. "What do—you—know—about him? Where's—he—from?"

"Settle down. It's a lead, nothing written in stone," my uncle said, lightly slapping my back. "If you're going to be a part of this, you gotta find a way to maintain your cool. I can't tell you things if you're constantly flying off the handle over every little thing we dig up. It's too dangerous."

He was right. I had to keep calm as much as possible if I hoped to find my mom.

"I got it. Really—I do." I put the glass on the counter. "Please tell me what you found."

He didn't respond immediately. Instead, he sat down at the bar and nodded toward the sandwiches. I perched on the edge of the wooden barstool. Taking a bite, he eyed me while chewing, obviously debating whether he could trust me with information.

Finally, he said, "Okay, this may or may not be what we're looking for, but a few months back one of my informants met another guy in a San Antonio jail who talked about a camp in West Texas, just this side of the border. He bragged to my informant that you could get cheap drugs there—" he hesitated, "and girls, too."

I mumbled a few curse words under my breath, staring at the sandwich in front of me. I tore it in half and fiddled with the crust. The good feeling I'd had while training earlier, and then hearing my friends were coming to see me, started to slowly leak out, like helium forced out of a balloon.

"It's not definite, but this dude told my guy about it. Said he'd accidentally bumped into the head boss while he was there. He hadn't talked to him, but he told my guy he was 'scary chill' but extremely paranoid, and he described him as having 'wicked mojo,'" Uncle Angel said, gesturing with air quotes, then shrugging. "Whatever the hell that means."

"From the way this dude described the operation and the boss, it could be our fourth coyote. Everything seems to be handled off grid, according to this guy. It sounds a lot like the trafficking setup your mom described to me," he said, wiping his mouth with a balled-up paper towel. "So, that's a solid lead we can chase, but there's more."

"My informant said one more thing. He told me homeboy hung with a gang that runs guns for a Mexican drug cartel. A big one. That means our fourth coyote may have ties with a cartel. Not great news for us, but it could explain how he has been able to work underground for as long as he has."

Gangs and trafficking and drugs? My mind began to swirl. I didn't know how we'd landed in this nightmare of a "Law and Order" episode, but I wanted it to end. I needed my mom out of it, safe at home with us. I couldn't change what had already happened or how these people had come into our lives. I had to focus on what could be done now.

"Do you need to let the police know about all this? About what your informant said? Can they help check it out?" I asked. "How can we find out who this anonymous creep is and whether he has Mom?"

Uncle Angel finished off his sandwich in two quick bites, then tossed the paper towel into the trash bin. He stood up, wiping his hands on his jeans. I watched him put lids back on jars and rinse the dirty utensils in the sink.

"The hell I'm letting anyone know anything right now. If my informant got his facts straight, this fourth coyote has some law enforcement in his pocket, too. So, we don't know who is involved," he said, looking over his shoulder at me. "Better to keep this off book until we know who and what we're dealing with. Safer that way."

There wasn't much else I could do but pray my mom was unharmed wherever she was. The not knowing scared the hell out of me.

"We're going to find her," my uncle said, as his phone began ringing. "Lemme get this. I'll keep working my contacts. See if anything else shakes out." I heard his voice drift off, as he answered the call, then he walked out back, the screen door slamming behind him.

I wanted to believe him, that part about finding my mom, but even if we did find this fourth coyote, whoever the hell he was, would it lead us to Mom? She had been gone so long. I watched him walk past my makeshift kick bag to the water's edge, a flock of mallards taking flight as he approached. He stood with his back to me, gesturing while he spoke into the phone, and suddenly a deep feeling of gratitude engulfed me. I leaned against the screen door watching him.

The realization of what he had done for us finally sunk in. He didn't have to stop that night to help us. And he certainly didn't have to keep us out of the system, give us identities, treat us as family, and watch after us for so many years. He'd put his career on the line to help me and my mom, not knowing how it would all play out. He was just a young officer when he'd found us, yet he'd risked his future in order for us to have one.

A moment later, while I thought about all he had managed, he turned back to look at me and gave a quick wave. I responded with a soft smile. For as long as I lived, I could never repay this man, *my uncle*, blood or not.

CHAPTER 19

Nine Days Missing

While waiting on Cici and Luka, I cleaned up, scrubbing my face and brushing out my hair. I didn't have time to shower, so I covered myself in a body spray Mom had left in a bathroom cabinet, something called Sparkling Spiced Pear. I sniffed at my wrists, pleased that I smelled like her. I'd given it to her two Christmases ago, but since she only used it here, more than half was left in the bottle. My happiness was brief, however. My moods flitted in and out, light and dark, indicative of my restless state of mind. Melancholy settled over me. What if this was as close as I'd ever get to her again? A fragrance in a bottle. A perfume that eventually would fade into nothing.

I forced myself to shake it off. I couldn't go there. Not right now. Besides, my mom would be unhappy if she knew I was giving into such bleak thoughts. She had taught me to have faith, even when things looked dismal, so that's what I'd try to do—trust that we'd find who'd taken her and that she'd somehow be okay. It was a tough ask, considering the circumstances, but I urged my brain to reroute to more positive thoughts.

First off, I was safe with my uncle in a cabin that was almost impossible to find unless a person knew exactly where to look for it. Most people didn't, so that put me at ease. And my best friend, a total girl boss, was coming here unexpectedly, which was a major plus. Especially since she was bringing Luka along for the ride.

By the time they knocked, I was in a more upbeat headspace. I opened the door, and Cici launched into my arms with a squeal. Seeing them here immediately lifted my spirits, my shoulder muscles relaxing instantly, like a measure of weight had been eased off them.

"Yummy! You smell good, girl," she said, releasing me and giving me a quick wink. Her grin told me she had come bearing good news. "We have so much to tell you!"

Luka stepped in for a hug, too, which I gladly jumped at. I probably held him too long, because he awkwardly tried to take a step back, but my body latched on for a few extra beats anyway. I had to pull myself away before I embarrassed myself. Yeah, I knew I was sending mixed vibes from the last time I saw him, but I was so excited to see them, I didn't care.

"Glad you made it. I tried calling you back after the call went dead but couldn't get through. I freaked when your phones went straight to voicemail, though. Guess I'm a little bit jumpy," I said, leading them to a worn leather couch in the living room. I plopped down in the matching chair. Uncle Angel had furnished the cabin with second-hand furniture, which was surprisingly comfortable despite its beat-up appearance.

"Yeah, we hit a dead cell spot, but we kind of expected it. We're officially in the boonies," Luka said with a laugh. "I didn't know this place existed! It's cool out here. I've never been east of Dallas. The pine trees are amazing—they're so tall, you can't even see the sky when you're driving on parts of the roads. It doesn't even feel like we're in Texas."

"Right? It's beautiful. And don't worry—we do get service here, but sometimes it's sketchy, you know? You gotta find just the right spot." I looked around the room, unconsciously picking at threads of the throw pillow nestled on my lap. "It's isolated, for sure, but that's why my uncle chose this area in the first place. To get away from the city. He and Mom love coming here. She likes feeding the chickens that the management company keeps on property. They're the cutest fluffy bantams. She'll sit out there listening to them clucking for hours. Says it relaxes her."

The two of them exchanged uncomfortable looks when I mentioned my mom. Luka coughed once, then focused on his lap, wiping his palms back and forth across the top of his jeans, while Cici examined the cuticle on her thumbnail like it was the most fascinating thing she'd ever seen. The room took on a somber silence.

Again, I pushed myself to shake it off. I cleared my throat. It was a fact. I missed my mom so much, any mention of her could send me down a dread-filled rabbit hole in seconds. My moods shifted so fast; it was difficult to stay on top of them. *Have faith*, I reminded myself.

I squared my shoulders, looking at them pointedly. "Okay. Hit me with it. What was so important you had to drive all the way out to 'the boonies' to tell me in person?"

Their faces immediately brightened, and they answered excitedly at the same time.

"We may have a lead on the gang members—"

"There's this attorney in West Texas who may—"

"Wait—wait. What?" I held up my hands. "One at a time, please. You have possible leads? Tell me everything."

Cici jumped in first. She leaned forward, elbows on knees. "We may have found a link between those gangster cases you sent us," she said in a loud whisper. "It's the lawyer! They all had the same lawyer associated with their defense. We found his name listed in each of the case files."

"The guy lives out in far West Texas," Luka interjected.

"Is it near El Paso?" I asked.

"Yeah, just outside the city," he said. "A tiny town barely on the map."

"Huh. Those gangs operate in and around El Paso, so I guess that makes sense," I said. "Okay? So, how does this help us?"

"Well, I kinda called him," Cici blurted. My eyes bugged out as I covered my mouth. "I told him I wanted to be a criminal defense attorney, you know, go to law school, blah, blah, blah. Told him I was working on a school research paper about gang-related cases and had stumbled on his name—"

"You what? You called a guy known to work with members of a criminal gang and possibly a cartel? What the hell, Cici?" Not to sound judgey, but the thought blew my mind. She'd spoken with a guy who was openly involved with and defended terrifying monsters, men who'd done despicable things to other people. They'd been convicted for raping, shooting, and killing others, not just some in rival gangs, but also young women like us. And Cici had been there when some scumbag actually *shot* at us. I'd asked her to research their cases, not pick up the phone and directly call a possible criminal.

"So, before you freak out, just know I covered my tracks. Like total coverage. I didn't give my real name or anything. I even said I was a student at El Paso High School, so he wouldn't know where I was calling from."

"She didn't. I was there when she made the call," Luka said. "She even bought a throw-away phone when she called him. So, no worries. It was all good."

"That was still too risky, Cici," I muttered. "These people are way out of our league, you know? We can't take unnecessary chances with these guys. I wouldn't forgive myself if something else happened to you.

Getting you shot at the other night when we snuck to my house, well, that was way too close."

"I know, I know. I get it. I promise," she said, glancing at the floor before smiling sheepishly at me. "On the bright side, my dad was able to get the car mirror fixed right away. So, there's that."

"Wait a sec. What night? Somebody shot at you? Who? When did this happen?" Luka asked. "Clarify, please. I don't understand what you two are talking about."

"Later, okay? I'll explain it to you on the drive home," she told him, then turned back to me. "Listen, I know it was impulsive to call that guy, but it's not only about helping you. If there's a way we can find your mom, I'm all in—as in one hundred percent. I love her, too, you know?" She paused. "Besides, you would do the exact same for me if it were my mom in danger. I know you would, so don't even try to deny it."

I choked up at that. Of course, I would. She knew me too well. It took a minute to get my emotions under control before I spoke.

"Okay, you're right. But, please, we have to be careful with this. We don't even know if the guy's involved beyond representing some really bad people. And when I say bad, I'm talking off-the-charts evil."

"True. But at first when I asked him about defense law, he was all ego about it, bragging about how many people he'd help get a 'fair shake.' How he'd managed to get many defendants off with much lesser sentences, yada, yada, yada," she said. "But when I told him specifically about these particular guys, the cases we were interested in, he got a weird sound in his voice."

"Weird sound? What do you mean?"

"His voice sounded strangled. He went from blowhard to mouse in like a second," Luka chimed in, snapping his fingers. "Like he was scared shitless. She had him on speaker, so I heard every word. We recorded it, too."

"Yeah. He couldn't get off the phone fast enough," Cici said, an impish twinkle in her eyes. Then she switched to a horrible British accent, adding, "Let me tell you, young lady, we're onto something with this guy. 'The game is afoot,' as Mr. Sherlock Holmes would say!"

I smiled at her attempt to lighten the mood, even though I knew this was no game we were playing. "What's his name again?" I reached inside my backpack, grabbing my notepad and hunting for a pen.

"Hill. Travis Hill," Cici said, her fingertips moving like lightning across the screen of her phone. "I'm sending you the recording right now."

I froze. The name, it rang a bell. More like it sounded a fire alarm inside my head. I began flipping through information catalogued in my brain. Then it hit me.

"Are you sure that's his name? He's connected to all of those cases I gave you?" I asked, a shrill, uncontrollable wobble in my voice.

"Yeah. Why? What's up?" The playful look in Cici's face quickly disappeared.

"I'm not sure." I forced my hands to work, pulling out the overstuffed file with newspaper clippings that I'd found hidden in our house. My fingers were shaking as I sifted through, looking for the article written about the first coyote's opening day of trial. I quickly scanned it and then placed it in front of Cici and Luka.

There was a quote attributed to the first coyote's defense attorney out of El Paso, who began the trial with opening remarks about his client's case. His name? Travis Hill.

"But I don't understand the link between this trial and those other guys you sent us? Is there a connection? How significant is it to your mom?" Cici asked after reading the newspaper report. I tapped my finger on top of the name and nodded.

"Yes, there's a strong possible link. Look, I can't explain all the details to you right now, but it's major." I jumped up from the seat and started pacing, then I abruptly stopped in front of them. "Okay, y'all, there's no easy way to do this. I have to tell Uncle Angel. He's the professional, and he'll know what needs to be done next. But I gotta warn you, since I didn't tell him I'd asked for your help researching the cases, he's going to be angry. Maybe even furious. It won't be about you. It'll be directed at me, full force."

They both stared at me, open mouthed. Then Cici made a face— she was familiar with my uncle's temper. Luka, who looked confused, had never met him before and had no idea what might come his way. He was about to get a snoot-full of Special Agent Angel Torres intimidation. But I had no choice. This information was too important for me to sit on.

I took a deep breath for courage and marched to the back door. My uncle was out back, standing by the water, texting on his phone.

"Uncle Angel," I yelled.

"Yeah?" he called, not looking up from his phone. "What is it?"

"Can you come in here for a minute?"

"I've got another call I need to make right now," he yelled back, sounding impatient with the interruption. "Can it wait?"

"No, it can't. We may have an important lead in Mom's case."

With that, his head popped up, and his eagle eyes zeroed in on my face. "Give me a second to finish this up. Be right there."

I hurried back to the living room and wedged myself between Cici and Luka on the couch. If I had to deal with Uncle Angel's wrath and/or his disappointment, I'd need some serious backup. Plus, the feel of Luka's knee pressing against mine boosted my resolve.

I heard the backdoor quietly shut and the sound of my uncle's light footsteps coming in our direction. "Okay, y'all. Buckle up," I whispered. "Seriously. He's gonna be pissed."

CHAPTER 20

Nine Days Missing

"Hey." My uncle stood before us with arms crossed, taking in all three of us on the couch. "What's this about? I don't have much time, so get to the point."

He openly stared at Luka, raising an eyebrow. "Have we met?"

"Oh! This is Luka, my friend from school. I told you he was coming," I said, a flush rising on my cheeks. My uncle could be embarrassingly abrupt at times, even borderline rude. "Uh, he's on the debate team with Cici and me." It was another reminder of how I had never mentioned a word about this boy to my family. How I had lied to my mother about how I'd been spending my time after school. I'm not sure I'd ever forgive myself for that.

"Uh, hello, sir. I'm Luka Fermi, I'm on the debate team with Mireya and Cici. But I guess she just said that," he said, as he stood up, a rosiness covering his cheeks, too. He reached out to shake my uncle's hand. "I've heard a lot about you, sir. It's a pleasure to finally meet you."

Uncle Angel studied Luka closely before he quickly shook his hand. Luka reclaimed his seat next to me, this time planting his right arm along the back of the couch, his body heat warming my neck and shoulders. My uncle looked at his watch, then at the three of us.

"So, you said something about a lead on my sister? I don't mean to be rude, but as Mireya knows, I don't have a lot of time to talk," Uncle Angel said.

"Could you first sit down?" I asked. "It's important. I promise.'

"C'mon, make it quick. I have people waiting to hear from me," he said, but finally sank down into the chair, resting elbows on his knees. He watched with a blank face as I gathered my thoughts.

"So, I, uh—after I found those files on those—um, men, I kinda—well, I passed their names onto these two."

He bounced up from the chair. Yep. I'd called it. He was fuming.

"Why in the hell would you do something like that? They don't need to be digging around in those cases," he said, his voice steadily increasing in volume. "I can't fucking believe you, Mireya! You weren't even supposed to be looking at that shit, now you tell me you're jeopardizing your friends' safety, too? This is not a stupid 'Scooby Doo' episode where the whole gang grabs magnifying glasses to go looking for fucking clues."

He clutched his head between both hands.

"There was method to my madness. Please. Just listen," I said, aware how he might see this as too risky. "Cici's mom is a paralegal, so she had access to more information than I did. I figured she could look into backgrounds, that's it. It's all done through a computer database. No one would even know she was looking into any of it. And Luka used LexisNexis at school, which also helped. You can search for individual court cases with it."

Before he could respond, Cici jumped in. "We found the name of an attorney who had represented those guys, he represented each one of the ones you were looking into over your sister's disappearance."

"So? That wouldn't be unusual. They probably all work with the same organization, which probably works with the same cartel, a group you certainly wouldn't want to tangle with," he said. "Do you understand what I'm saying? These are seriously cruel people who do horrific things, especially to little girls like you."

Cici and I flinched. My uncle had made his point.

"Excuse me, sir, but I believe they're aware how dangerous this is. I don't think any of us is taking this lightly," Luka said, his debater voice level and confident. He would make one hell of an attorney one day, I thought, sending a small smile his way. But it quickly disappeared when he added, "That's why Cici used a throw-away phone when she called him."

"Called him? Cici *called* him?" Uncle Angel looked at me with bulging eyes. "For the love, Mireya—you and your friends are going to get us all killed!"

"Wait, sir, listen for a second," Luka said, his voice still calm. "She pretended to be an El Paso high school student working on a research paper about criminal defense. That's it. With a fake name and a phone that she tossed, there's no way he could trace that call to Cici. Well, it's highly unlikely, anyway."

My uncle strung curse words together under his breath. He frowned at Cici, and through clenched teeth, said, "What exactly did he say to you?"

"Well, that's just it. The minute she asked about those specific cases, he got scared and ended the call," I said, standing between him and my friend. "And there's more. The name of the attorney she talked to? Travis Hill. Does that ring a bell?"

"Wait. The same guy who represented the coyotes in the trafficking trial?" he asked. "Are you sure?"

"One hundred percent," I said.

He stood silent for a moment, processing the information.

"That means it's likely this attorney knows the fourth coyote, as well, since they ran in the same circles," he said, almost to himself, rubbing the back of his neck. He looked down at the flor, his haggard face shadowed, as he shook his head. "How could I have missed that? I must have read the trial manuscripts a hundred times. But I never tied that defense to these possible suspects I've been investigating."

"Because you're exhausted. And so am I. It never hurts if you have fresh eyes on a puzzle, right?" I glanced at the two friends now at my side, filled with pride. Maybe what they'd discovered would help. Maybe it would push us in the right direction toward my mom.

Uncle Angel sighed.

"I owe you an apology," he said. "That's a solid lead. Impressive work. Even though you took a huge risk doing it."

"Thank you. I know it was kinda crazy calling that guy, and we really don't want to cause any more drama than you all already have. We just want to help find Ms. Torres any way we can," Cici said, shrugging. "Mireya's the one who connected him to this other trial you're talking about. She hadn't told us anything about that."

"It's a long story," he said, "maybe we can share another day. But, right now I need to go make some calls about what you've told me. The reception is much better out back."

Cici eyed me, then in a barely perceptible move, lifted her chin toward Luka, who inclined his head slightly. I wouldn't have even caught the exchange if I didn't know my best friend so well.

"Mind if I go, too? I need to call my mom. Let her know we made it here, so she doesn't worry."

They headed out back in a discussion about cell providers, leaving Luka and me behind. My mouth suddenly felt dry. He stood so close; it became difficult to catch my breath. He seemed to take up all the oxygen in the room. I hesitantly moved to the front door, not sure what to do with myself inside.

"So, like I was telling you earlier, the property management keeps all kinds of livestock on the grounds. Wanna go see the chickens?" I asked, opening the screened door and stepping outside. It was a beautiful day in the 80s with hardly a cloud above. "They're just around the corner. You gotta see how cute they are."

"Sure. Lead the way," he said, with a playful grin. "I'll follow you any-where." Mhmmmm. Apparently, there wasn't enough oxygen outside either.

"Wow, you weren't kidding about that uncle of yours. He's uber intimidating, yeah? I was about to pee my pants," Luka said. He ducked under a low-hanging branch and grabbed a handful of leaves as he passed. "I sure wouldn't want to be on the wrong side of that dude."

"No, you wouldn't," I said with a chuckle, glad to be thinking about something other than how attractive Luka was. "He's the closest thing I've ever had to a father. I'm lucky to have him."

"Even if he scares the bejeezus out of prospective boyfriends?" Luka asked, his eyes crinkling at the corners as he smiled.

"Especially if he does that," I tossed back at him. He snorted. I couldn't help myself, even though my nerves were zinging all over. I loved flirting with this boy. He made me happy.

"Well, come to think of it, he's not that terrifying," he said, reaching for my hand. My heart flip-flopped as our fingers entangled and our arms swung in a gentle rhythm. "I could take him, if I had to."

"Yeah, right. I wouldn't be too sure about that," I said, breathlessly, breaking into another goofy grin. "He may be older, but he's wily."

We walked side-by-side, teasing each other good-naturedly. I could hear the gentle *clucking* coming from the chicken coop as we neared. The sounds reminded me of Mom, but not in a sad way this time. We stopped in front and watched about two dozen chickens of varying colors in constant motion, trilling and chirping to each other as they busily went about their business.

"I know you're not in the right headspace for a relationship. I got that loud and clear the other night," he said out of the blue. "But when or if you're ever ready, I'll be around."

With that, Luka brought the back of my hand to his lips and pressed a chaste kiss against my knuckles. A bolt of electricity pulsed through me, my knees almost buckling. But I didn't want to run this time. Maybe I'd allow myself this—a few moments of feeling goodness in the world, warmth and love, instead of the secrets and danger and ugliness, in which I'd mostly been surrounded of late. Maybe that simple kiss, which burned my skin and turned my knees to jelly, was enough for me in this time and place. Maybe it was enough to help me have faith in happy endings again, something I wanted to believe in for my mom's sake. And for mine.

Chapter 21

Eleven Days Missing

B linking sleep out of my eyes, I wrestled with sheets and blankets to free myself from the bed. Two days had passed since Cici and Luka had been here, but the afterglow of their visit (and Luka kissing my hand) had faded sometime in the middle of the night, replaced by an anxiousness that gnawed at my brain. Maybe it was because forty-eight more hours had passed without much progress, making it eleven days Mom had been missing. Uncle Angel couldn't locate the attorney who Cici had spoken to. It seemed the guy had disappeared from the face of the planet after her call. Not good. Not good at all. Restless with that knowledge, I hadn't been able to turn off my thoughts.

I pushed off the edge of the bed and steadied myself. My mind was fuzzy, my peripheral vision frayed at the edges. I shrugged a lightweight hoodie over my PJs and pocketed my phone, stumbling into the bathroom where I splashed cool water on my face, then quickly ran a brush through my hair. I resembled an unmade bed, I thought, as I peered closer into the cloudy mirror. Who was this person? God, I needed to tweeze my eyebrows, trim the frizzed dead ends in my hair. Simple tasks that I hadn't bothered with since this nightmare started. I made a face in the mirror. I'd take care of it sometime soon. Maybe.

I made my way to the cabin's tiny kitchen in about three steps. Uncle Angel had left a note by the stove. I read it then tossed it on the counter. He'd be back soon. He'd gone to get us more groceries at Kent's Bait Shop, a local dive that also served as a market/bakery/diner. It was about a thirty-minute drive from here. My mouth watered—maybe he'd bring back some of those yummy kolaches they baked in the store. I quickly texted him about grabbing us a dozen, but the phone service was temperamental again. The text wouldn't go through. Figures. I'd try again outside.

I slipped the phone back in my pocket, yawning as I poured myself a cup of hot coffee, leisurely stirring in cream and sugar. It was nice to have a little time to myself without Uncle Angel constantly hovering. He kept working to find my mom—keys constantly clicking on his laptop or stealing away to the best areas for phone reception to make calls. I loved my uncle, but his OCD tendencies drove me nuts. Plus, his restless energy wore me out. The constant taekwondo workouts helped a lot, but I could barely handle my own restlessness, much less his obvious anxiety. It was amazing that I had never noticed that about him before.

I looked out the kitchen window, watching two geese land in the serene lake, the birds barely causing ripples on the smooth surface. Mom loved taking the canoe out there, where she'd pull up the oars and simply drift on the water, leaning back with a good book, letting the current take her wherever. Some of the most relaxing times we'd had together were quick getaway weekends here with my uncle. We'd spray down with insect repellent and take off on kayaks, usually early in the morning hour before the heat squelched the fun. It was low-key, where we were surrounded by the soft trilling of roaming chickens and goats *mah-ing* and *baa-ing* in their pens. My mom was in her element here. She enjoyed slipping sugar cubes or baby carrots to the horses kept on the grounds, speaking to them in hushed tones while she nuzzled their necks, the horses crunching their treats in glee. And because she adored it, I did, too. I loved seeing the glow in her cheeks, her easy smile, none of her usual defenses set. Here, she seemed free, almost like a young girl.

Out on the lake, an older man in a canoe caught my eye. He cast a fishing line out, his back to the sun, his face a silhouette. It was still cool enough to go outside before the heat settled in. With mug in hand, I slipped out on the porch, letting the screen door bang behind me.

I lingered on the top step, inhaling deeply, soaking in the sharp, rejuvenating scent of pine trees that surrounded the cabin. Things around me came into crystal clear focus. Sunshine warmed the tops of my cheeks, and the gentle sounds of nature lulled me into a deep stillness I hadn't felt in a while. I slowly released a deep breath. A spark of happiness bloomed within me for a moment. The peacefulness of this place was like a salve to my soul. Then an unknown voice shattered the calm.

"It's a beautiful place, huh?" A man was sitting on a wooden bench about ten feet from me, under the shade of a tree. He wore a blue blazer, sunglasses and his light-copper hair was combed back with gel, making it look like the head of a Ken doll.

I froze on the wood step, which creaked under my weight. An adrenaline spike killed my peaceful buzz. What was a stranger doing outside our cabin? Did it seem like he'd been waiting for me or was I being overly paranoid again? Maybe he was another visitor here, although most people at Spotted Fawn Lake didn't wear sports jackets on their morning walks. It was more of a holey-tee-with-cut-off-jeans kinda place.

"Uh, yeah," I said, as I slowly retreated up the steps, creaking again. "Beautiful."

"No, no, darlin'. Trust me, you don't wanna do that," he said, tossing a casual smile over his shoulder. He patted the seat next to him on the bench. "C'mon. Sit down here, right next to me. Enjoy this spectacular view."

I turned for the door but stopped mid-lunge when I saw another man blocking it. He was shorter, beefier, and not dressed as well, but also wore dark sunglasses. A large, black pistol rested in a holster at his hips. My stomach sank. I considered my options while staring at the gun, but realizing I had none, I turned back and trudged toward the stranger on the bench.

I sat down, the coffee in my cup gently rippling like the lake water in front of me. My fingers wouldn't stop trembling. He eyed the cup before yelling over his shoulder.

"Hey, Robert, pour me some java, huh? And put a couple teaspoons of sugar in there if they have it. But only if it's real sugar. None of that fake shit." He leaned back, untroubled, grinning at me. His large teeth were electric white, and something in the curl of his lips reminded me of someone I knew. I considered throwing hot coffee on his dimpled cheek and making a run for it, but he must have read my mind, because he coolly pulled out a gun, using the barrel of it to scratch along his jaw.

"This is pleasant, huh? Peaceful. It's nice to take a little break, connect with nature—breathe in fresh air for a change. Lemme tell ya, running a business gets to be a pain in the ass, ya know. Everyone's always bitching about something—the shipment's late or it's not what we ordered. Blah, blah, blah. But this?" He nodded toward the water, which lapped quietly against the shoreline. "This I can get behind."

My knee started bouncing as thoughts began racing. I could scream or try to make a run for it, but with the second guy behind me and both men carrying weapons, I wouldn't get far. I was trapped. And I wasn't sure, but these had to be the guys who'd taken my mother. The thought stabbed at my heart. She had been trapped, too.

The screen door slammed from behind, then the man named Robert appeared with a steaming coffee mug for the guy next to me. I could feel him watching me behind mirrored lenses as he handed over the cup. Then he retreated to the porch to resume his post.

"Thanks." The stranger next to me put the gun in his waistband, crossed his legs, and delicately blew on it before taking a sip. He acted like he was used to others serving him, as if he was entitled to it, which made me hate him even more. Then it hit me suddenly. I knew who he was because I recognized him from the sketch. The fourth coyote—the mastermind from years ago—sat right next to me.

"Hmmm. Good coffee, huh? Did you make this?" he asked, smacking his thin lips together. "Not a bad cup o' joe, little lady. Not bad at all."

He looked out over the water, casually waving to the old man in the boat, who returned the greeting, obviously clueless that I was in physical danger and that the man next to me was a wanted fugitive, not to mention, a living monster. I pushed my hand in my pocket and lightly tapped the back of my phone three times, turning on my voice memo record button, the way I had found on YouTube a few days ago. I hoped it was recording properly. I hadn't planned for this scenario, especially not here and now, but I was improvising. I prayed this guy hadn't noticed.

I swallowed hard, trying to find my vocal cords.

"Who are you?" I asked softly. "What do you want from me?"

A small laugh escaped him as he side-eyed me. I wasn't in on the joke. He paused and took another sip, like we were two friends casually chatting at a coffee shop.

"So, I understand it now," he said, nudging me with his elbow, followed by a knowing grin. He placed the mug on the ground next to him and draped an arm along the back of the bench, almost touching my shoulders and causing the tiny hairs along my neck to rise in protest.

I couldn't deny it. Being this close to pure evil was intimidating, like standing at the edge of a volcano that could erupt any second. I eased forward, away from the heat of him, as best I could. "I couldn't figure out what she was trying to protect. I mean, I knew she had information, she always had key details about my operation, but there was something else I could never put my finger on. Something much more valuable that she didn't wanna share."

He couldn't stop smirking. Then he cackled and slapped the top of his knee. Not only was this man wicked, but he was also fruit loops. A bad combo, for sure. I itched to wipe at the perspiration under my neck, but I was too afraid to move.

"And now I figured it out. It was never a *what*." He turned to me, beaming. "It was always a *who*. Fuck me! Can you believe it? *A who*!"

This animal had taken my mom. He had all but said it. I clenched my jaw muscles, blinking back the sting, trying to figure out what in the hell he was going on about. *What* and *who*? All I wanted to know was who he was and what he had done with my mother. I needed her to be alive. She needed to be okay. And I had to find a way to get out of this mess, or at least stall him until my uncle came back, because he definitely had the upper hand with his gun and his armed goon behind me.

"Where is she? I want to see her." I gripped the cup tightly on my lap. "Did you hurt her?"

"Who? Ana María? That's what she goes by these days, right?" He scoffed, brushing off his slacks. "Me—hurt her? No, no. You won't pin that on me, darlin'. She chose her end years ago. She all but took her own life the day she chose to run, and then reveal things to law enforcement that she knew better than to share." He peered thoughtfully at me through dark shades. "Wow! That seems like several lifetimes ago, ya know? I s'pose it was."

My chest tightened. I could barely pull oxygen into my lungs. He was responsible for my mom's disappearance, and maybe much worse. If only I could use the coffee cup in my hands to bash that arrogant smile off his face, maybe crack open his head. I wasn't a petrified child anymore, afraid to act. I could fight back this time. But how many seconds would I have before one of them shot me? How far could I get before one of their bullets sliced me through the heart and took my life? I couldn't find her, protect her, if they killed me. I had to stay alive and figure out where she was. I had to be smart.

"Who—the fuck—are you?" I said with all the fake calmness I could muster. I couldn't let him know how afraid I was.

"Lord, where are your manners, girl? Someone has a foul mouth. Did Ana María teach you to talk like that? It's really no way to speak to an elder." He took off his sunglasses, showing kaleidoscope eyes, an almost exact reflection of mine, except the colors in his appeared flat, lifeless, like a reptile's gaze. "Or maybe you'd rather just call me Daddy?"

I gasped as hot liquid sloshed out of the cup onto my lap. *Oh, God, no. Not him. Anyone else but this jackal.* Then I buckled over and vomited coffee-colored goo on his fancy, leather loafers.

CHAPTER 22

Eleven Days Missing

Each time she looked at my face, Mom must have seen him, the eyes of the beast responsible for kidnapping her and her sister, imprisoning them, forcing them into sex trafficking. He had destroyed their lives, caused her sister's death. How had she done it? How had she managed to look at me full of affection? Because that's all I'd ever felt from her my entire life. Never anything but love. I couldn't imagine the strength she possessed to see me as more than just an extension of the animal sitting next to me now.

Nausea wracked my body. I couldn't believe he was my father, except for his damn eyes. I couldn't deny the similar pattern and the exact colors as mine. I had wanted to know my father for as long as I could remember. Since I was old enough to understand that I didn't have one because he was dead. Or so I'd been told. But this person? *No.* I didn't want to know *him.* My life had taken on the plot twist of a Greek tragedy.

"Try to contain your joy," he said mockingly, as I continued to dry heave next to him, my head wedged between my knees. Unfortunately, I had nothing left in my stomach to spew at him. His shoes were covered in coffee and yellowish sick.

In a calm voice, he called over his shoulder, "Robert, grab some towels, huh? Quickly. She nailed my Ferragamo's. What a mess."

I wiped my mouth with the back of my hand and slouched against the bench. If I wanted to save my mom, I had to keep it together. I needed to record him telling me something, anything that connected him to her disappearance. We needed evidence to nail his ass for all he'd done to my mom, to her sister, to those other nameless innocents he'd poached from families and put in cages. All so he could make money off the depraved.

"I don't know who you are," I said, looking at the coffee stain on my lap. "What's your actual name? As for calling you Daddy, forget it. That'll never happen. Hell will freeze over first."

"Don't be stupid. You know I won't give you my name," he said with a chuckle. It wasn't funny. Not even close. I decided I'd call him "Snake." That seemed fitting for the piece of excrement beside me.

"Did you—are you the one who took her?" I silently prayed he hadn't already killed her.

"Of course not." He raised his eyebrows and shrugged as if he couldn't have cared less, adding, "I have people for that."

The arrogance. The casual indifference. Nausea was replaced by fury, igniting in my belly and electrifying my limbs. My fingers balled into fists. I felt an urge to shove his face under the lake water before us and hold it there. I could visualize the bubbles escaping his lips, feel him struggle helplessly to breathe, watch his lifeless body sink below once he took that last breath of water. Maybe there was a part of him, a sliver of monster, that lived inside me. Maybe this apple hadn't fallen far from the rotted tree.

Robert rushed over with towels and a bowl of water, squatting down to carefully dab at the sick-covered shoes. With his head bent as he cleaned, he paused to take off his sunglasses, darting a look my way. We briefly locked eyes, and that's when it hit me. He was the bastard who'd shot at me and Cici. And it occurred to me why he'd looked familiar that night when I saw him in the side mirror. Robert was one of the faces in the many mugshots my uncle had in those files. My gut told me he was one of the men who abducted my mom, too. I considered grabbing the gun from his holster, but it was on the opposite side, farthest from me. I'd never make it, and as much as I wanted to chance it, I couldn't risk it. If there was the slimmest possibility Mom was alive, I had to tamp down the anger threatening to consume me. I had to find out more.

My top priority was to keep Snake talking. Given the heartless way he spoke, he was obviously a sociopath, which meant he was probably a narcissist, too. I figured the viper would enjoy bragging about how superior he was to the rest of us.

"So, how were you able to grab her in the middle of a town square in front of God and everyone? I'm not sure how you did it, but it was impressive to pull that off." I pressed my lips together as tightly as I could to keep them from curling in disgust. "But I don't understand why you would risk it? What did she ever do to you?"

"What did she do? That's a fair question. She crossed me and then attempted to rub my nose in it. Not something I take kindly to," he said, with a placid smile and frosty glance. "Actually, it was an unwise thing to do—not something I'd expect from her, of all people. But surely, she told you about it? Her plan to blackmail me? How she sheared me for thousands over the past year?

"If she'd had a clue, she would have stayed hidden," he said, with a wink. "I'd given up years ago that I'd find that bitch, then one day, out of the blue, she contacts me, all cloak and dagger."

I didn't believe him, but then again, my mom had hidden those bundles of cash. And she'd stashed fake passports along with them. So, I guess that's where all the money had come from? But why had Mom decided to blackmail him now, after so many years? The only thing I could figure was she needed it to pay for cancer treatments. Maybe she'd been desperate and couldn't find another way to cover the medical costs. It was the only reason that made sense.

"Thank you," he said pleasantly to Robert, who had finished cleaning his shoes and again retreated to the porch.

Snake stared at the canopy of trees overhead. I tried to edge away, but he draped his arm behind me on the bench again. I flinched as he rested his hand on my shoulder this time, then pulled me closer.

"She should have remained hidden. I mean, what on God's green earth was she thinking? I'm guessin' she got greedy, like everyone else. Disappointing, really—I always thought better of her, ya know?" He sighed. "If she hadn't contacted me, threaten to go to the authorities unless I paid her off, I probably never would have found her. Dumb move if she thought I wouldn't eventually track her down. An unfortunate twist for her, I s'pose."

He squeezed my shoulder even closer. My mind raced for a way to get out of this. A way to save both my mom and me from the serpent next to me.

"Ah, well, the woman you call Ana María—not her real name, by the way—always had balls of steel," he said with a snort. "I gotta give her that. She was a tough one."

I gritted my teeth. The way he spoke about her in past tense rattled me. But I focused on what other useful bits I could pull from him.

"What was her real name?" I asked.

"Doesn't really matter," he said, with a dismissive wave.

"It matters—" I said.

"Like I said, she was ballsy and smart. I liked that about her," he said, speaking over me. "That's why I gave her so much latitude in the operation. She was a go-getter—quickly worked her way up."

"Wait. What are you saying?"

"Yeah, before she crossed me seventeen years ago, I trusted her with—how shall I say this—the delicate aspects of the business. She procured the finest specimens for me. Was damn good at it, too. Had an eye for the beautiful, broken types who'd respond to her approach. She was quite skillful, really, once I—shall we say—gave her a little push. The drugs helped take the edge off her, so she'd do as she was told. And threatening to kill her family—well, that didn't hurt either." His fingertips ate into the flesh of my shoulder, as he shot me a scornful look of surprise. "She really never told you she worked for me? Huh. So, tell me, what did she reveal about her youthful indiscretions? What secrets did she share with you?"

Procured things. Did that mean what I thought it did? I refused to accept what he was suggesting. He was a liar. My mom was one of the kindest people I knew. She helped everyone. There was no way she'd be involved in his despicable business, unless she'd been coerced.

"I don't know what you're talking about." I avoided his gaze. "My mom teaches math to middle-school kids. You have the wrong person. Let her go."

"For the record, your mother never taught math," he said. "Now," he paused dramatically, "the woman you know as Ana María may have, but not your *actual* mama."

God. I hated the possessive way he spoke my mom's name, like he knew her. Like he owned her. A blinding anger erupted from me. I could barely distinguish the features of his repulsive face so close to mine.

"Stop talking about her like you fucking know her," I suddenly snarled, startling him. It wasn't the smartest play, yelling at a man with a pistol, but I couldn't control my temper. He brought out the worst in me. Maybe because he *was* the worst of me. "I know what you did to her back then, and what you did to her sister, my birth mother. They were just kids when you raped them and pimped them out, you twisted douchebag. I'll kill—"

He moved fast, grabbing a handful of my hair and yanking my head back hard. "Shhhhhh. Now, now, play nice, darlin', and show Daddy some fucking respect," he said, his warm breath in my ear. My neck felt like it might snap, and a pain like liquid fire seared my scalp. I struggled but refused to scream. He placed the barrel of the gun in the nook of my collar bone and lightly tapped. "That's one ugly temper you got there. It'll get the best of ya if you're not careful, little girl."

Stay calm, Mireya. Stay alive, I heard my mother whisper inside my head. I closed my eyes, listening to my own ragged breathing. Then an unexpected stillness settled over me, encircled me, a tranquil feeling like when my mom would hug me close and stroke my hair. My heart rate slowed. Everything in my life with Mom became clear. She had trained me for this moment since I was a child. This was her greatest fear, that this monster might come calling one day. So, she had taken it upon herself to prepare me for him or anyone like him. Maybe because she hadn't been ready when he'd come for her so long ago.

"Now, there's a good girl. Best stop," he said, interrupting my thoughts. "No one likes a talky bitch who doesn't know when to shut up."

I channeled all the survival lessons my mom had taught me over the years, as well as all the self-defense skills I learned in taekwondo classes. All the tips I'd picked up from my uncle. I could do this. I was capable of protecting myself and the ones I loved. She'd known all along that I could, even if I hadn't. I'd figure out how to free myself, maybe even hurt him if I could. It would require mental discipline, but I could do it. I'd stay patient and look for the exact moment to attack. I emptied myself of rage and sadness and all emotions that would distract me. I mentally detached from the situation. Then I turned a blank, steady gaze on him.

"Go on," I said.

"Right. So, as I was saying, Ana María acquired some beautiful creatures for me, including your birth mom. She was one of the finest of all, one of my favorites, in fact." He smirked at me, as he slowly loosened his grip and used the same hand to smooth down my hair. My nostrils flared, but I tried not to flinch at his touch. "You know, you should smile more often. Maybe fix yourself up some. You could be just as pretty as she was."

I refused to react, letting his words pass through me. He hunted and sold girls, young women, probably boys, too. Drugged them, imprisoned them, forced them into sex acts to line his pocket with dirty money. He was the lowest type of lifeform. As soon as I was able, I would squash him under my heel like the cockroach he was. But I needed clarification on what he'd just said, no matter how painful it was.

"Back to what you were saying before. I'm not sure I understood. Are you saying my mom—uh, Ana María—brought girls to you? Like, she actually helped you kidnap them? Is that what you mean?"

"That's exactly what I mean. Ana María was no saint. Far from it. I s'pose she was innocent when I first found her in Albuquerque. I'd taken a wrong turn, and just happened upon this lovely vision walking home after school all by her lonesome. So trusting, that one—she hopped right into my car when I stopped to offer her a lift. Of course, she was scared outta her mind once she realized she wasn't going home, but it didn't take her too long to learn how to stay alive," he said, relaxing slightly, but keeping an arm around me. "She met your biological mom—her name was Michele—outside a convenience store in Durango, Colorado, I think it was. Ana María was my right-hand man back then. She had this knack for earning their trust so fast. Amazing, really. Girls trust other girls, ya know, even if they're with older guys who drive. They'd all but leap into the car, so eager, wanting a ride to the mall or a fast-food joint. But, instead, she'd bring 'em straight to me."

His wide grin and creepy snicker revealed how much joy he took in telling me this. The amount of hatred I felt for this man—I struggled to hide it. His words slipped deep into my heart as if he'd slid a dagger through flesh. My mom, the woman who had empowered me as a young girl and as a woman, had worked with a sex trafficker? A predator? How could she do that? Everything I thought I knew about her, everything I believed in, seemed to be a lie. My heart wrung in my chest, like I was having a heart attack. Or maybe a panic attack. Who could tell? I wanted to curl into a ball, call it quits. I wasn't sure I could fight for someone who'd brought innocent girls to this lowlife. Daughters not much younger than me who'd had families who missed them, who'd had entire lives ahead of them before being captured and imprisoned in tents in the middle of nowhere.

He had a smug twist to his mouth as he studied me, as if he could sense the conflicted reaction inside my brain. It seemed to thrill him to deconstruct everything I knew about my mom—to tear down the image I had of her and spit on it. But that was how most criminal psychopaths operated. I had to remember that.

No. I refused to believe what he'd said. It wasn't that simple. There was more to my mom's story—I felt it in my bones. I didn't care what he said, there was no way my mom would have willingly helped this pathetic excuse for a human unless she'd been threatened or drugged or tortured or all of the above. I absorbed the pain of those possibilities and forced another question through dry lips.

"But weren't my mom and Michele sisters? I thought they were taken together. As a pair."

"Sisters? See, kid, just another example of Ana María's lies! They acted like sisters, true, but they sure weren't related. Michele was a stunning blonde. Hot as hell. Lord, I couldn't get enough of her myself back then. Her parents were Polish, I think, as in they had *actually* moved to the states from Poland. Cool, right? Professional skiers or some shit like that." He stared at the lake as he spoke. "Michele was in great demand. But Ana María developed this thing about her, tried to protect her from the clients who sometimes got a little rough. Her bullshit was bad for business, though. She forced me to teach her and Michele a painful but vital lesson—keep the customers happy. Period."

God, I couldn't believe this subhuman creature had fathered me. As best I could, I maintained an impassive face, but inside, I was seething. I silently counted to twenty before speaking again.

"Michele was only thirteen years old, though, right? Was my mom telling the truth about that?"

"I s'pose when she first came to me, she was." He made a face and shrugged. "But who cares? She didn't look thirteen."

I winced. His voice was disinterested, the response of a man comfortable with doing unspeakable things. Innocence would mean nothing to him. He defiled it as easily as he had combed back his plastic hair this morning. I had to move on before I lost my cool again.

"How did you find us out here? Nobody knows about this place," I said, changing the subject. "My uncle made sure we weren't followed."

Snake slapped his knee and laughed.

"Follow you? Now, why would I do that?" He cocked his head and winked. "After that stunt you pulled a few nights back, we were easily able to hunt down the driver, you know, that hot little friend of yours. Robert memorized the car plates before you two blew outta there, smokin' tires and shit. Made quite the exit, huh? But it didn't take too long to find out where she lived, ya know, plant a GPS tracking device on the car. Had to wait a few days, but it was just a matter of time before she led us to you."

My body tensed, my face tightening. A roaring noise began in my ears. He knew where Cici lived? Had been tracking her whereabouts in the car? My fingers curved into claws on my lap.

"Did you kill my mother?" I snarled. "Ana María? Did you kill her?"

"Don't concern yourself with that. She's been dealt with," he said smoothly, covering his mouth to cover a small yawn. "So, here's the situation. This walk down memory lane has begun to bore me. I'm a busy man, and you and me, we have important matters to discuss."

She's been dealt with. Words that could easily translate into *I killed her.* I stared at the dark stubble on his neck, the small spot just above his carotid artery that he must have missed shaving. He casually rubbed at it with the back of his fingers.

"Now, I have a much more critical question. As I asked earlier, what did Ana María share with you? Tell me about your mother-daughter chats. What did she tell you about me? Give me all the juicy details."

"That my biological father died before I was born. That it was a brief, unhealthy relationship." My mind moved toward spiraling into despair at the possibility he had killed her. I wrestled to keep it from pulling me into the dark abyss of agony. Instead, I willed myself to focus on him, waiting for the right moment to break free. "That's it. That's all she ever said."

"Well, she had half of it right." He exhaled a disappointed sigh. "But I really don't believe you. I think she told you all about my operation and where she stored all the dirty details. That's why you went to the house the other night, right? You went in there to grab the thumb drive that she'd threatened me with—the one she said she'd stored everything on."

"So, here's what's gonna happen. First, you're going to give me that thumb drive, get it from wherever you might have squirreled it away. We figure that's why you snuck back to the house—guess you got to it before us. No way I'm going down for shit that happened years ago. I intend to stay unknown and underground, if you get what I'm saying. Once you give me what is mine, we'll determine if you live or die. Understand?"

I didn't answer. I had no idea what thumb drive he was talking about. He stood, pulling me up with him. I realized he wasn't much taller than me when we were standing next to each other. Then, a surprised grunt sounded from the porch, startling both of us as we turned toward the noise.

My heart soared as I took in Uncle Angel ambushing Robert from behind, his arm wrapped around the man's neck and a gun shoved into his side. Robert stood gasping for air, his face a brilliant shade of scarlet.

The time was now. I lunged away from Snake's grasp and moved into a challenging stance. He wouldn't shoot without getting that thumb drive, information he thought I had. My open hands were before me, my weight distributed on the balls of my bare feet. I'd sparred opponents in countless tournaments, but never had the prize been so important to me. I'd never wanted to destroy an opponent as much as I wanted to put an end to this man.

"Tell me where she is, and you get the fucking thumb drive," I said, deadly soft. "What have you done with her? If you've hurt her, I'm going to kill you."

He rolled his eyes and laughed with disdain, reaching for the pistol under his waistband. So maybe he would shoot me. What the hell did I know?

The first rule I learned in self-defense training was that it's almost impossible to fight against a gun. So, summoning all the fighting skills in my arsenal, I swung my leg around, sending a roundhouse kick that sent the pistol spinning through the air, before he had the chance to point it my way. I sprang back.

"You're quite a spitfire, alright. Just like Ana María," he said through a forced laugh, straightening up and brushing off his pants. "But things didn't end well for her, either, I s'pose."

He was baiting me. Before I could respond with more kicks, a tussle erupted on the porch between my uncle and Robert, who had somehow managed to break free and knock the gun from Uncle Angel's hands. In the two seconds I was distracted, Snake wrapped a hand around my wrist in a vice grip and jerked me to him, then circled his other hand around my neck and squeezed, long and hard, as I frantically clawed at his fingers, struggling to suck in air. My vision dimmed, and I felt myself gravitating toward unconsciousness, but my uncle's voice broke through the darkening haze, giving me a moment of clarity.

"Break away, Mireya!" Uncle Angel yelled, as Robert aimed the weapon at him. "Run!"

At that moment, I realized something about myself. My mom hadn't raised me to run. She had raised me to charge. I was bigger and bolder than these small men. I would not let them take another person I loved. Even if I died trying to stop them. I fought more, wriggling my neck out of his grasp, just enough to gulp in oxygen.

Using my body weight and a sharp jab to his ribs with my elbow, I twisted free of Snake's hold and whirled away from him. He watched with surprised, wild eyes, holding onto his side. Then he spotted the gun nearby on the ground. It looked like he was calculating whether he could get to it before I got to him.

A profound wail of rage that had been submerged inside me since they had taken my mom rose to the surface. Without waiting another second, I hurtled toward him, swift and graceful, a shriek piercing the air, as I cried for all the daughters, mothers and sisters who'd been chained, violated, and silenced. All for what? For the perverted desires of lesser humans like him.

In taekwondo, I was taught to focus all my mental energy on the point of contact. The mind was the most powerful tool we possessed, I had learned through the years. It enabled us to break a two-inch-thick board or a slab of cinder block with our bare hands.

So, I focused on his most vulnerable point—the eyes. It was a painful blow forbidden in tournament sparring, but it was needed right now. I forcefully whipped two fingers into his left eyeball, darting away, as he screamed in agony, swiping at me. A rivet of red ran down his cheek, and I flicked away the blood on my fingertips, as if it were a dead mosquito's.

"Shouldn't have done that, you fucking bitch," he raged, both of his palms covering the wound. "I'll kill you myself—slow and painful. You're all mine now."

"That's where you're wrong." I danced before him, my hands in a defensive position in front of my body. "I'll never be yours. Only hers."

I slowed everything down inside my brain, directing my focus on him, my entire being in tune with his every move. Patiently I watched, ignoring the tussle on the porch. Filtering it all out as I considered his body's next greatest weakness at that specific moment in time.

"And *this*? This is for her," I said, as I rushed him, flying through air, concentrating all my mental energy into the side kick planted dead center on his crotch before he had time to react. If it had been a board, I would have made a clean break, snapped in two. He whimpered in surprise, moaning, crumpling to a fetal position on the ground, as I flitted away.

I chanced a look toward Uncle Angel, who had resumed the upper hand in his fight. He watched me with his mouth agape as he held Robert face down in a stranglehold.

"Damn. You're a badass," he said, a slow grin spreading across his face. But suddenly his face contorted into fear, and he yelled, "Watch out, Mireya!"

I felt the Snake's body collide into mine from behind, but I twirled away from his momentum, just barely. He righted himself. I guess my mom wasn't the only one with balls of steel. I wasn't sure how he'd come back from that last strike. It took down most men.

"Something you need to know. When we were torturing your mama, you wanna know what she kept screaming?" He sneered, unable to straighten his stance, his eye unhinged, his face covered in blood. He looked demented, which he was. "She told me she couldn't stand the sight of your face. It reminded her of me." He cackled, before bending over in a coughing fit. He attempted to pull himself together, adding, "She said she'd wished she hadn't taken you. Her biggest regret, she said. You weren't ever worth dying over."

That just proved he was a liar—he hadn't known about me, that she'd run away with a baby, who happened to be his daughter, until he'd seen my eyes today. Besides, I knew my mom had never said that, never would. He was about to say something else but stopped. Maybe I looked as demented as him.

I returned his insane smirk, then lunged, coming at him on his left side, weaker because he couldn't see as well. I slammed the edge of my palm in a knife-hand strike to his carotid artery, which knocked him to his knees. He gasped for breath, then passed out in a heap at my feet.

I leaned over him, ready to strike again, wanting to. One downward blow would kill him, crush his windpipe, like a crumpled soda can. It would be so easy to rid the world of him. For her, for my birth mother, for all those nameless faces he'd preyed upon. I wanted it so much I could taste it—to put an end to this piece of shit, so he'd never hurt another person again.

I drew back my elbow, eyeing the windpipe sticking out of his neck, just begging to be smashed to bits. But I paused. Inside my head, I heard Mom say, *Taking his life, it will only burden yours, mija. Don't give him that.* I breathed in and out, weighing my desire for vengeance against what my mom would expect of me. An inward debate raged, as I weighed the pros and cons of letting him live.

My arm went limp in the end. She was right. Taking a life, even as pathetic as his, was too much weight to carry, especially if I didn't have to. I'd make sure he went to prison. From what I'd heard, inmates hated child predators. Maybe they'd take care of him in their own way. That would be my revenge.

I reached over and slapped at his slack, bloodied cheek, making sure he was really knocked out.

"Just like you said, Snake," I muttered under my breath, "no one likes a talky bitch."

CHAPTER 23

Eleven Days Missing

The county sheriff's officers arrived at our cabin about twenty minutes after the old fisherman called 911. He'd watched the fighting from his canoe out in the middle of the lake—where, apparently, he had decent cell reception—then came to shore to help Uncle Angel subdue Robert, who continued to thrash about despite being pinned underneath my uncle's weight.

"What in the world is this all about? You folks okay?" the old man, whose name I later learned was Mr. Pettit, asked as he shuffled toward us with frightened eyes, carrying an oar from his boat. He paused in front of me, lanky with a bent back, staring with admiration. "Never seen anything like this here karate kid. You're something else, young lady."

He made his way over to my uncle, gesturing with the oar toward Robert, who grunted loudly on the ground like a caught animal. "Want me to smack him upside the head with this thing? That'd shut him down quick."

"I think I got him," Uncle Angel said, "but I appreciate it."

"Too bad," Mr. Pettit said, stepping near, and jabbing Robert's bloodied cheek with the tip of the oar. "Always wanted to do something like that. Sure 'nough—beat the holy crap outta the likes of this one. Like one of them action heroes in the movies!"

Both Uncle Angel and I were speechless, and a worried looking Robert tried to wriggle his face as far away as he could from Mr. Pettit and his prodding oar. We raised our eyebrows, locked gazes, then erupted into uncontrollable laughter, that hysterical kind that hits when people realize just how close they'd come to dying.

"Thank you again, sir, for helping us," my uncle said to the older man, when we finally stopped laughing.

"You kiddin'? This is the most excitement I've had in a decade or so," Mr. Pettit said, grinning. "Just wish I coulda whacked him, is all. From what I could see, he deserves every bit of that and then some."

Snake remained sprawled out beneath me, but, just in case, I kept my foot pressed hard against his ribs. If I saw the slightest movement, I'd gladly use Mr. Pettit's oar to knock him out again, six ways from Sunday. I studied his appearance, noting the damage that I'd delivered—a torn, bloodied eyeball half dangling from the socket, along with deep reddish-purple shadows blossoming on the sides of his face and along his neck. It was difficult to see any resemblance to me, but then again, he looked like he'd been beaten with a baseball bat. With any luck, he would never see properly out of that left eye. That was my hope, anyway.

I pulled out my phone and hit the 'stop recording' button. I prayed I'd captured everything he'd said, every word, so the police would have evidence that he was behind my mom's disappearance—and God knows how many others.

When officers cuffed his hands in front of him, he was still unconscious, drool pooling out of the corner of his open lips. Battered but alive. EMTs lifted him onto a gurney and placed him in an ambulance, which left with lights flashing and tires crunching down the gravel road.

It was followed by another ambulance that carried Robert. His nose and cheek looked to be crushed, and the EMTs said he'd suffered a punctured lung. My uncle had done his own damage, it appeared.

After being examined in an ambulance, Uncle Angel and I were cleared. We'd both suffered cuts and bruises—including blossoming purple marks in the shapes of fingers that encircled my neck—but other than that, we were okay.

We answered countless questions, as officers took photos and poked around the yard. They also interviewed Mr. Pettit, who offered his own account of what had happened, which made me out as quite the badass. *Thank you very much, Mr. Pettit.* When the sheriff's deputies finished interviewing him, we helped him into his canoe, thanking him profusely for his assistance. We stood watching him slowly paddle away, making his way toward his cabin across the lake, and waving as he turned to look at us one last time. It was then, as Uncle Angel pulled me into a tight embrace, I cried.

We had won the battle against the monster, but we still had no idea where my mom was. It occurred to me that I might never know. I now realized I could survive without her protection if I had to, but that didn't mean I wanted to. I'd much rather she was standing here next to me. Always.

As if he could read my thoughts, Uncle Angel whispered against my hair, "Don't worry. We won't give up searching." He pulled back and brushed tears off my cheek. He leaned his forehead on mine the way my mom always did. "You were *fierce*—just like her. She would have been so damn proud watching you hand his ass back to him. I know I am, Mireya."

I tried to smile. She would have been ecstatic to watch me take that snake down. I eased away from my uncle's embrace. I had to ask him the question, no matter how tough it might be to hear his answer.

"Be honest." My voice trembled. "Do you think she's still alive? Or do you think he killed her? He said—" I could barely get the words out, "she had been—taken care of."

He looked away, at a point beyond my left shoulder, his lips tightening into a slim line.

"I don't know." He exhaled. "I want to believe she is, but I really don't know. We don't have evidence showing us one way or the other."

I gulped back emotion, running a hand along my tender scalp. He didn't need to elaborate.

When he looked at me again, his eyes shone with resolve. "But whatever happens, I promise you this. I'll do everything in my power to make sure that scumbag gives us what we need to find her. And that he pays for his crimes. Each and every one of them."

We stood, arms linked, squinting at the lake. The sun had climbed directly above us, and the glare of its rays bounced off the water like sparks of liquid diamonds. Birds called to one another from the shelter of trees, and insects hummed. It was so peaceful; I didn't even mind the perspiration that beaded above my lip or the stickiness at my back of neck as the heat intensified.

"They'll still have questions for us," Uncle Angel said, his gaze following the flight of a lone crane overhead. Yes, they would. The investigators would have lots of questions. Like why had the missing coyote resurfaced after so many years, showing up at our lake house? And if he had taken my mother, what was his motive for doing it?

We quietly discussed the situation we now faced. I had to make sure Uncle Angel didn't get into trouble for helping my mom and me all those years ago. Who knows what would have happened to me if he hadn't stepped in to help us. At first, he'd argued that he needed to turn himself in, but I pleaded with him. I couldn't lose him, too. He reluctantly agreed, and we made sure our stories synced.

About a half-hour later, Detectives Anderson and Cho arrived in an unmarked cop car. They had made it here in record time. Uncle Angel had called them right away to report Snake's attempt to take me. I forwarded my cell phone recording of Snake to them (there was nothing that would incriminate Uncle Angel on how he had broken laws giving us new identities) and fielded another round of endless questions. Poker-faced, they'd scribbled down answers in their notepads.

"Were you aware your mom knew the perpetrator? Did you know your mom had been trafficked as a teenager? Did you know this man was your father?" Detective Anderson asked.

"No, no, and no. I did not. She never spoke about anything like that," I answered. Technically, that was not a lie.

Uncle Angel hugged his torso, and shook his head no.

Detective Cho peered up from her notebook, asking both of us, "Did she still have connections to this—what are we calling him? —the fourth coyote? Had she ever mentioned him before?"

"Not to our knowledge," I said. "We don't even know his name. He wouldn't tell me. I'm not sure how he found her after all this time, or what exactly she has on him." I took a sip of water from a bottle the paramedics had given me. "Said she was demanding money from him in exchange for her silence about his past operation, but I don't know. I can't believe anything he says. He's insane."

"Huh." Uncle Angel cleared his throat. "Have you found anything on the money my sister had in those accounts? Any connection to any dirty money?"

"No. There's no trail at all. It's as if it just appeared there in cash deposits over the past year, but we haven't found a trail to anything. Not, yet," Detective Anderson said, watching both of us closely.

And on and on. The questions they'd asked Uncle Angel and me seemed never-ending, but we sidestepped them as best we could. The toughest one was when they asked my uncle how, as her brother, he hadn't known she'd been abducted by a sex-trafficker. It was a legit question. My uncle's shoulders slumped as he considered his response.

"It's complicated," he said, wiping a hand over his brow. He shot me a miserable look, then answered the detective. "I was older and wasn't around much. Had moved to another city and barely kept in contact with the folks. Personality clashes with my dad, that kind of thing, you know? I knew she had run away from home, but that's all. She never confided in me about that time in her life. There were certain things Ana María kept to herself. She's always been an extremely private person."

He paused, looking off at the lake before tugging on his right earlobe. I reached over and grabbed his hand, leaning in closer to my uncle.

"As far as the family knew, she ran away, got pregnant, then came home with this one," he said, letting go of my hand and putting his arm protectively around me. "That's it. It happens all the time. If I had been a better brother, though, I would have made her talk to me more about what she'd gone through. I regret that."

They seemed content with our responses at the moment. Detective Cho's phone rang in her blazer pocket. She slipped it out, eyed the number, then answered.

"Yes. Okay," she said quietly, walking away from us. "He say anything, yet? Hold off as long as you can on that call. Yeah. We'll be right there."

She ended the call and nodded at her partner.

"Looks like he's conscious," she said. "Hasn't said more than two words. Won't give his name and didn't have identification on his person. He's asking for an attorney, some guy in West Texas they haven't been able to reach, yet. Maybe we can have another try at him before the lawyer shows up."

"Yeah, maybe we can interview his henchman before he lawyers up, too," Detective Anderson said. "Let's get a move on."

We'd talk more later, they said, then they took off in as big a hurry as when they'd arrived. The elusive fourth coyote's name was still a mystery, along with the whereabouts of my mom. I cursed under my breath. Why hadn't mom named him in her journal? Maybe she tried to distance herself from the trauma she experienced. Or maybe she was simply petrified of him. After meeting Snake face-to-face, I could see how frightening he could be.

Uncle Angel led me into the cabin, poured some cold coffee and heated it in the microwave. He went to his car and came back with a box of kolaches from the bait shop. He warmed those, too, and my stomach growled in response, even though I didn't feel hungry.

"C'mon. Drink and eat up," he said, sliding a mug and plate in front of me at the bar. "You'll need your strength. We have more work ahead of us."

The aroma spurred something inside. Suddenly, I was ravenous. I shoved half the apricot kolache in my mouth and chewed, savoring every delicious, crumb.

"That was some kinda crazy today, right?" I toyed with the other half of the kolache. "Thank you for having my back."

"I've always got your back," he said between bites, then wiped away the crumbs from his mouth with a napkin. "And I know you've always got mine. Your mom would expect no less from either one of us."

True. She wouldn't. We continued eating in silence with a mutual understanding—we'd never stop searching for her or seeking justice against those who took her. We'd always have her back, too.

CHAPTER 24

Thirteen Days Missing

Turns out Snake's real name was Shelton. Shelton Donald Krueger II, but folks around town called him Donny. No wonder he'd preferred the nickname Ojos Locos, which translated as "crazy eyes." It certainly would have packed a mightier punch with the criminals with whom he associated.

"So, his last name is like that serial child-killer in those wacko horror films from the 80s? The guy with the blades for fingers?" I'd asked Uncle Angel after he told me the latest. We sat at the kitchen table in his house, the same spot where I had confronted him with Mom's go-bag and cash. That day seemed ages ago.

"Yep. Spelled just like that freaky dude in 'Nightmare on Elm Street.'"

"Figures." I'd buried my head in my hands. Regardless of the guy's real name, he'd always be Snake to me. "Has he given us anything on Mom? What about that man Robert? Anything from him?"

"Nada. Neither one of them has said a word, except to ask for their attorney, who arrived at the jail yesterday. The same guy your friends tagged. Thankfully, that recording you made has linked Krueger to her disappearance or else we'd have zero to go on," he said. The skin under his eyes looked smudged with charcoal. I wasn't sure when he'd last slept. He had been mostly gone since we'd captured Snake and Robert two days ago. Cici and Luka had stayed with me most of the time, so I wouldn't be alone.

"But I'm working with undercover officers from various agencies plus a network of my own sources, trying to see what we can find," he continued, reaching for my fingers, and squeezing. "We'll find her. I think we're getting closer. Try to keep the faith, huh?"

I nodded, but any hope I had dwindled with each day that passed. It had been almost two weeks since she had been abducted. Two weeks was an eternity in her situation. Would they keep her alive or just get rid of her? Did she have any leverage left that we didn't know about? And, if so, where would they have taken her?

My dark thoughts were interrupted by Uncle Angel, who shared more details about Snake. Apparently, he had gone to a private university in Dallas, majored in business, where he met and married his wife. The couple had twin sons, which meant I had two half-brothers, new information that I honestly couldn't deal with right now. After graduating from college, he had returned home to take over the family's sprawling ranch outside of Del Rio, a place among the acacia and cacti that peppered the southwest Texas brush country. Rumor had it he'd never had interest in the business and had quickly driven it into the ground. So, it appeared he'd started a side hustle in sex trafficking to prop up the family operation, Uncle Angel's sources said. Nice family guy, that Donny.

He may have sucked at ranching, but it seemed he thrived undetected as a sex trafficker. No one would have suspected he operated clandestine portable houses of ill repute on his ranchland or nearby, across the border, moving them constantly to keep from getting busted. He also dabbled in human smuggling, working with coyotes to bring immigrants illegally across the border. No one would have suspected that Donny

Krueger—upstanding church elder and Pony League baseball coach of his twins' team—was Ojos Locos, who paid off authorities on both sides of the Rio Grande to keep their mouths shut. That's probably how he had disappeared off the radar as the elusive fourth coyote so many years ago, Uncle Angel said.

Among the citizens of Del Rio, Donny was a longtime resident from a wealthy family who hosted an annual community charity ball along with his wife, a former Miss Texas. Each year the power couple raised millions for children's missionary work in Africa. They were beloved by the community for helping so many children in need. That fact made me gag, the bitter irony of it all.

But to the underbelly of society in the area, Ojos Locos had earned a reputation for being one nasty, unstable dude. He was known as extremely paranoid and often erratic. Rumor had it if he heard even the slightest murmurs that someone had spoken about his operation, they'd either disappear or their dead body would be discovered off some desolate, county road, hundreds of miles away.

"They're searching the ranch and surrounding area as we speak, in case he's keeping her there," Uncle Angel said, blowing on the steaming mug in his hands. He was on his third cup of coffee, and it was only eight o'clock in the morning. "Sounds like the wife was clueless about his lucrative side business. But we're seizing everything—paperwork, electronics—to see where it leads us."

I stared at the wooden table top, tracing the winding grain with my fingertip. *What if we don't find her? What then? Where could she be?* I gulped down a lump of panic. My left eyelid started involuntarily twitching, and my knee bounced in sync.

"Uncle Angel?" I choked out, unable to look at him. I allowed myself a moment to feel like a small child, not the ferocious young woman who had attacked the bad guy and kicked his ass.

"Yeah."

"You said they're searching right now?" I paused, having a difficult time forming the next question. "Are they using the cadaver dogs?"

He put down the mug, pulling me up from the table and into his arms. He held me for a few minutes, then released a sigh above my head before answering.

"Yes, they are, but, listen, that's how this always works. It doesn't mean it's the worst-case scenario."

I sobbed into his shoulder like I did when I was a child. This man who wasn't my blood relation had been there for me since as long as I could remember. An uncle, a father, a big brother, a protector—all rolled into one. He had stumbled upon my mother and me in the middle of the desert almost eighteen years ago and had risked his career to help us. He also had changed the entire course of his own life. Whatever happened, I could never repay him for what he had sacrificed to help a left-for-dead young woman with a newborn child clutched to her breast.

"Hey, I love you Uncle Angel," I said into his shirt, my voice raw with gratitude. "She—loves you—too."

"I know, mija," he said, his voice breaking, his head resting on top of mine. "I know."

***

It was days later when we received official word. Authorities had stumbled upon a barn in an isolated section of the ranch, where they seized about three hundred pounds of brightly colored fentanyl pills, a fifty-five-gallon-drum full of liquid fentanyl, and more than two hundred pounds of crystal methamphetamine. Quite the illegal drug stash for such an upstanding citizen. They'd also discovered an old-school ledger that connected him to selling those substances, as well as his human and sex trafficking operations. Snake would go down for drug distribution and, if a few witnesses flipped on him, which Uncle Angel believed they were likely to do, he'd also get nabbed for trafficking crimes.

My uncle and I celebrated the concrete evidence that was building up against him.

But our excitement didn't last long. We still didn't have a link between him and my mom's abduction, other than the recording I'd made, which might not nail him on a charge. The authorities had combed every corner of his ranch and other properties but hadn't found a single trace of Mom—dead or alive. Not one physical clue that she had ever been taken there.

It was as if she'd disappeared into thin air after that morning at the ATM. One minute, she was a living, breathing image on a surveillance screen, then *poof*, gone without the slightest trace. No one could explain it. She was nowhere to be found.

CHAPTER 25

Eighty-Four Days Missing

Mom turned thirty-six years old, and we gathered to celebrate her. That's if the day we've always celebrated was the actual date of her birth. There was a chance it wasn't. Our lives had been built on secrets, upon more layers of secrecy, on top of a foundation of falsehoods. She and I had lived inside the proverbial house of cards, I suppose, that could have toppled if a single truth had been revealed. It was difficult to tell what was fact and what had been fabricated to keep us safe, to protect that foundation. If I were a young woman on the run, I certainly wouldn't have used my actual birthday on fake documents. But that was me. I'd asked Uncle Angel about it, but he'd sheepishly shrugged and said he wasn't sure either. It was the date she'd asked him to put on the papers he'd assembled for our new lives. That was all he knew for certain.

Maybe it'd be more accurate to say we were *honoring* her today. If I were to get technical, there wasn't much partying going on. Not at first, anyway. Both Shilpa and I had burst into tears over the decorated cupcakes she'd made, and Cici, who had planned the gathering at my uncle's house, took one look at us and immediately began sobbing, too. The cry fest lasted a good five minutes while Luka and Uncle Angel stood nearby, with stoic expressions and hands crammed into their pockets. It might as well have been a funeral.

"I'm—so sorry—Mireya," Cici said, struggling to get words out between sobs. "I thought it would be—a good idea to gather together—you know, to remember her special day and all—but it's too—it's too painful."

"Hey, it's okay, really. She would appreciate this, and so do I. All of it," I said, as I wrapped my arms around my thoughtful friend, who saturated the top of my shirt with her tears. "It's just I'm sad she's not here to see it—that's all."

Cici always spoke about my mom in present tense, bringing her into our conversations. I appreciated that simple gesture. Most of the people I talked with these days either stumbled with words when they mentioned her, or they didn't say anything at all. It wasn't that they didn't care. But discussing our situation seemed too difficult, especially since my mom had been taken by violence, and no one knew whether she was alive. Folks, in general, had no clue what to say to that. I got it. If I were them, I'm not sure I'd know what to say either.

I did make a speech on my mom's behalf at the gathering. I knew if she'd been there, she would have thanked them for coming, for being there since the beginning of this mess, and for supporting each other while we continued to search. So, I sucked it up and strung those words together, ferociously blinking back tears as I spoke.

Then I added, "Mom always felt weird about being a younger mother. Like she was being judged by the other moms, because she'd been a teen when becoming a mom. Most of them were older women, who had careers before having children, stuff like that." I sniffled and swiped at my nose. "It makes sense now, but at the time, I didn't get it. In my mind, I thought she'd wished she would have waited to have a kid, you know, that she'd wanted to live a more exciting life before getting saddled with me."

"But that wasn't the real issue. It was that past life I never knew about. Maybe it was because she always had her guard up around other moms, keeping secrets and probably feeling inadequate because of the things she had experienced. I don't know. All I know is she was a kid when she took me in, a girl who'd been through a hell we'll never truly know or understand, if we're lucky, but who stepped up to help another girl's child have a good life. She could have run without me that day, and countless days after that, but she didn't." I stopped speaking, pausing to look at each one of them. "She is the bravest person I know, and looking around this room, that's saying a lot." I raised my soda can in a toast. "So, here's to finding her. She never gave up on me—and I'll never give up on her."

"To Ana María," they answered around the room, not a dry eye among them.

Everyone hung around afterward. Shilpa had brought two heaping plates of spicy potato and pea samosas, along with a chicken and rice dish warming in the oven. We ate, drank, laughed, and cried some more, as we sat around my uncle's kitchen table, working on a thousand-piece jigsaw puzzle. Later, we pulled out the Scrabble board and played a game—another one of my mom's favored activities. I tried to stay present with them, tried not to let my mind wander, wondering where she was at that moment, praying she was alive, hoping she knew we were still looking for her.

While the others gabbed in the kitchen, washing dishes and cleaning up, Shilpa and I sat side-by-side at the table. It made me happy that she'd come today—especially since she barely left her house since my mom's disappearance. The puzzle, which, of course, was one of my mom's favorites, spread out in front of us, almost completed. The image showed a circle of adult female elephants helping a new mom with its little one, each one supporting the baby with its outstretched trunk. It was beautiful to see the teamwork that went into raising their young, a fact that had fascinated my mom.

Admiring the photo, Shilpa leaned her slight shoulder against mine. I inhaled a whiff of cinnamon from the hot chai in her mug. She took a sip of it, as she tapped a fingernail on a cluster of pieces showing one of the adult elephants by the baby.

"This reminds me of Ana María. Not just the puzzle, but this photo. She used to wonder why men would hunt such lovely, intelligent creatures. A tragedy, really. So often they'd slaughter a herd, leaving mutilated carcasses behind, taking only the animals' tusks." She shook her head, lips pursed. "'Shilpa,' your mom would say to me, 'They're so much more than ivory.'"

"Yes—so much more," I said.

My mom had taught me that, too. There were humans who only valued their ivory tusks, ignoring what made elephants extraordinary—their complex matriarchal society; their intelligence, curiosity, and long memories; their obvious loyalty and love for one another; how the females banded together to protect their young; their ability to grieve and feel empathy for others; the wisdom they shared from generation to generation; even their fear of tiny bees. Now that I knew about Mom's past, I better understood her feelings about these magnificent creatures. They were kindred spirits, underestimated for their value and what they brought to the world. Like my mom and other victims of trafficking, they were unjustly taken, abused, and eventually discarded because some men valued a limited part of them.

"I want to find her family, Shilpa. Her parents, if they're still alive, and any brothers or sisters. Reach out to them and let them know." She took my hand and squeezed it between both of hers, as I continued, "I know what it feels like to be in the dark, not knowing what happened to the person you love. I hope she's back by the time I find them. Then we could go together if it's safe for her. She could see her family again."

"She would love that," Shilpa said, dabbing at watery eyes with the edge of her sleeve. "I'll help you in whatever way I can."

My mom's parents—whoever and wherever they were—had been missing someone they loved for more than my lifetime. I couldn't imagine waiting that long and never knowing. The same applied to my biological mother's family. She was someone's missing child, too. One of millions who'd been snatched by evil and never found. I'd begin looking for her family, too, using the details Snake had revealed the day he tried to kill me. It wasn't much to go on, and he'd probably been lying, but whatever. It was a start.

And there were so many more families—with parents like Gary, my fellow searcher who'd lost his son—still searching for their kids, hoping for any clue of their whereabouts, needing to know if they were dead or alive. It was overwhelming. There didn't seem to be a way to protect them all, these children, and yet, I still wished for a world that could.

I studied the pieces before me, looking at shapes and colors, attempting to distract myself, catch my breath. But it was difficult. My chest squeezed, as I tried to process the untold number of children who'd disappeared like Gary's son. Like both of my moms. Almost a half a million children went missing each year in the United States alone. If not for Mom coming to my rescue when that random woman tried to take me at the mall when I was a child, I might have become a statistic, too. But she'd made sure that I learned how to protect myself in case I faced that danger again. It was a small step in an overwhelming problem, but it made the difference for me when Snake had come calling.

Then an idea came to me. Maybe I could make a difference for one child. Or five. Or twenty. Or maybe even more. I realized I couldn't protect each one, but I could do what my mom had done with me. Prepare as many of them as I could. Teach them to defend themselves if they were to ever need it. I would contact my taekwondo instructors and ask if I could teach a special self-defense class for the little ones, as well as the teens.

"What is it?" Shilpa asked, interrupting my thoughts. "You're so quiet, my dear. What are you thinking?"

The others were still chatting in the kitchen as they cleaned. I heard the sounds of silverware clinking, and the water faucet turned on and off. I inhaled deeply as I studied the puzzle before me, finding a piece, and clicking it into place. I turned to Shilpa with a confident smile.

"It's just—I've thought of a way I can help other kids like my mom," I said, telling her about my idea. A hopefulness filled me, as I explained my plans, and it seemed to light up Shilpa, too. "Is it a crazy idea? What do you think?"

"Are you serious? That's a brilliant," she said, clapping her hands together. "Ana María will be so proud of you! You are so much like her—trying to make this world a better place."

If I were to go back in time, I'd try to defend those two young girls who were my mothers. Unfortunately, I couldn't time-travel to warn them or shield them from what was to be, nor could I protect my mom from getting abducted at the ATM that morning. But maybe, just maybe, I could help girls and boys who might encounter predators in the future. If I could pass on to others the gift my mom had given me, maybe I could make a difference like she had. Maybe it would be like I was protecting her from the scumbags who had preyed upon her young self. Even if it meant just one less child went missing, it would be enough.

I settled back in conversation, as the others rejoined at the table, bringing bowls, spoons, and cartons of ice cream with them. Mom would have loved the gathering, and I held onto faith that next year she'd be able to celebrate her birthday just like this. It would have been a perfect day—except she wasn't with us. That part sucked.

While I was sitting with everyone, the phone in my pocket buzzed with an email notification. I had set it to notify me, so I wouldn't miss a call, text or email from police or anyone regarding my mom. I froze when I saw the message, the phone wobbling in my hands, then dropping, cartwheeling in slow motion to bounce off the tabletop.

"Oh my god, Mireya." Cici was wide-eyed, scared. "What? Is it about your mom? Did they find her?"

It wasn't about my Mom. It was about me. The genome testing company had my genetic report ready for viewing. And one more thing—I had a DNA match.

CHAPTER 26

Eighty-Four Days Missing

My fingers trembled as I clicked on various buttons to get to the DNA section of the ancestry site. I had almost forgotten I'd taken the test—the company had sent a message apologizing for taking longer than usual to process the saliva sample I'd submitted three months earlier. Yet another thing I had hidden from my mom. At the time, which now appeared laughable, it had seemed so important to find out more information about who my dad was. But since then, my life had been distorted in every which way. Hell, if I was honest, it felt as though I'd transformed even at the molecular level. My priorities had long since shifted.

I could feel everyone holding their collective breath, as they huddled behind me. Uncle Angel lightly rested his palm on top of my shoulder, a soothing pressure that reminded me I wasn't alone. I paused before touching the button that would take me to the genetic match, sucking in a deep breath, and slowly puffing it out. My face felt clammy. My fingertip hovered above the blue digital rectangle appearing on my phone screen.

"You okay?" Uncle Angel asked, his voice gentle from behind. "You don't have to look at it right now, míja. You've had a lot thrown at you. Do what you need to do, and on your own time. There's no pressure."

"No—I really want to know," I said, my voice squeakier than usual, "but—I'm afraid. What if it's someone on my father's side? I don't know if I can handle more bad news about where I come from. I never dreamed I'd be the daughter of a deranged psycho, and yet, here I am."

The irony. For years, I'd dreamed of learning more about my biological father, not knowing that he'd actually turn out to be a wanted criminal—a monster who hunted and ensnared young people, selling their bodies for money. Let's not even get into the circumstances in which I'd been conceived, and how my biological mother had been not much more than a child when she gave birth to me. What if I had more relatives like good ol' dad on the family tree? Was it possible the family DNA—that 0.1 percent that made each of us unique from other humans—had a genetic predisposition for that kind of personality? If so, did I want any part of that lineage? I wasn't sure I could process more potentially negative information from that side of my genetics. Having more than one Snake in the family tree could possibly do me in.

"I understand you're afraid, but you're nothing like him, regardless of what DNA you may share," Shilpa said, her voice soft but firm. She carefully turned my face to hers, her thoughtful eyes inches from mine. "But there's another factor to consider. Maybe you're more like her—your biological mother, I mean. There's a fifty-percent chance this match is from her family, no? You wanted to locate them if you could, let them know what had happened to her, right? What if this person leads you to them?"

True. It could open a door to the other side. To the biological mother I knew nothing about and whose parents, if they were living, might still be looking for their daughter. I owed that to her, and to myself, really.

I turned back to the phone screen, pressing the button as fast as I could so I wouldn't wimp out. The match popped up. It was a woman who shared about twenty-five percent DNA with me. On the *maternal* side. Tears sprung to my eyes. After studying the information on statistical breakdowns, it looked like my biological mother had a sister. I had an aunt. I clicked on her icon and saw the photo of an attractive, thirty-something woman. The oval shape of her face, the full lips, the slight bump in the nose, all of it looked like an older, similar version of me, except with wavy blonde hair.

"Oh my god," Cici shrieked behind me, jumping up and down next to Shilpa, who placed a hand over her mouth. "Look. At. Her. Can you believe it? This is amazing—yeah?"

I stared hard at the photo, soaking in each detail of her face, the pleasant curve of her smile, the crinkles at the corner of her eyes. I had never looked anything like my mom or my uncle. It was strange seeing a similar face looking back at me. Strange, but exciting. The possibilities surged in my brain. But not all of them were positive.

"I'm just—I don't even know what to think," I said, blinking at the screen. There was so much to absorb.

I studied the ethnic breakdown of my results, and then what ethnicities I shared with the woman, my DNA match—most of it was Swiss, Austrian and Slovenian. The other half of me, Snake's side, appeared to be mostly a mix of Irish, English and German. No Latin blood at all, not even a touch, according to the results, which cemented the genetic truth, harsh though it was. It made it quite final, without a doubt. My mom had never been my blood relation. But she'd always be my mom. I didn't care what a genetic test showed. And this other woman, this newly discovered aunt, would I feel any connection if I were to meet her? We shared DNA, yes, but what if we shared nothing else—no bond, except partial chains of double helix. I shook my head to clear it.

"What should I do?" I said, thinking aloud. "I'm not sure what the next step is."

"Message her," Luka said, moving in closer, pointing to my phone screen. "My dad did this recently. Met a cousin he hadn't known about. After he got the match, he sent a message to the guy. Now they're texting about family genealogy and stuff."

I looked at the icon of the woman's account. There was no name, just a way to send a direct message via the site. It said she'd last viewed her account two weeks ago. How did I go about contacting someone who had no clue that I existed? Who probably had no clue what had happened to her sister. My stomach tightened. Would she welcome hearing from me? Or would I represent something horrible, the dark truth of what had happened to her lost sibling? I was older than my biological mother had been when she'd disappeared. How could I explain that I knew next to nothing about her? Only that she had died giving birth to me, or that was the story I'd been told. And what other details I could share about the trafficking ring wouldn't make for a pleasant story, either.

"I don't know if this is a good idea—she may hate me," I said, my eyes starting to water. "What if she blames me for her sister's death? I mean, I'm alive, but her sister is gone."

Luka squatted down, wrapping a protective arm around me, pulling me close to his chest.

"No one could hate you," he said, his voice barely above a whisper. "None of this is your fault. What happened to her sister, and to your mom, those events were set into motion long before you came along.

You had no control over what they experienced. They were victims of multiple crimes. That's not on you, Mireya."

I knew he was right—none of it was my doing—but still. Having to tell this woman what had happened to her loved one—and, oh, by the way, I happen to exist because of the torture she endured—well, that was heavy. I wasn't sure I knew how to explain it. And, if I had to, I certainly didn't want to do it via a message. It was a story I'd need to tell her face-to-face, a tragedy that would be almost as brutal for me to relay as it would be for her to hear.

"I don't know if I'm strong enough to do it," I said, staring at her photograph. "What happened to my biological mother and my mom after they were taken—it was beyond horrible."

"Strong enough? Are you kidding me?" Uncle Angel said. "Yes, you are strong enough. I watched you take down a monster with no weapons on you—only a quick mind and your hands and legs. It pisses me off that what happened to them is part of your story, Mireya. It sucks. It really does. But if anyone is strong enough to share it, along with your Mom's and your biological mother's stories, it's you. I'd stake my life on it."

The support I felt around me, surrounded by those who loved me, fought for me, who had lifted me up when I could barely stand emotionally, gave me strength. I thought of the leader of the group searches, Gary, another person who had buoyed me these past months, who would have given anything to know what had happened to his boy, even if the details crushed him. I would do it for all of them. For my moms, for their families, for those around me, for Gary, and, yes, even for myself. I could share their stories, even if I struggled through the telling. Their stories mattered, and so did mine.

"Okay, I can do this," I said, with a resolute shake, "—but I'll need each of you with me. First thing, I'll need to write a note introducing myself. That's it, nothing heavy. Then maybe see where that takes us. Sound good?"

They all agreed. I opened the messenger file and began typing.

"Hey, looks like we're related!" I typed to the stranger. Maybe it sounded lame, but before I could overthink it, I pressed the send button. It lacked flair and imagination, but whatever. That's all I could come up with right now. It was a start.

CHAPTER 27

One Hundred Twenty-Five Days Missing

J abbing at the tall weeds with my pole, I inched forward in the chain
of searchers combing a wooded property east of Dallas, just off
Interstate 20. We were looking for signs of a fifteen-year-old girl named
Jordan who'd been catfished on the internet by a predator. The man, a
doughy fifty-something with a combover, had posed as a sixteen-year-old
boy, according to direct messages later discovered on Jordan's gaming
account. He'd set a meeting place at a convenience store near her house in
the suburbs, northeast of the city. The store's surveillance camera caught
young Jordan—sporting cutoffs, a pink tee, small hoop earrings and
freshly glossed lips—climbing into his waiting SUV. It was the last image
anyone of her alive. Two months had passed before police found and
arrested him in Shreveport, Louisiana, after he'd attempted to abduct
another girl. The only signs of Jordan they'd found were a few red strands
of hair on the passenger seat of his vehicle and a single gold-hoop earring
buried under the floorboard mat. Authorities believed he had raped and
killed her, before dumping her in the wooded area, based on information
he'd given and the records they'd obtained tracking his phone usage.

I forcefully stabbed at the weedy area around me, as I thought of the scumbag, another Snake-type stealing the lives of their young victims. I wished for twenty minutes alone with him, so I could make him hurt like he'd made that poor girl suffer. During the months I'd been volunteering with Gary's search group, I'd heard similar stories over and over, and although it ripped my heart each time we conducted a search, unsure of what gruesome scenes we might stumble upon, I'd done it for the families. Each time, I laced up my hiking boots and took a pole in hand for them. They deserved to know what tragedies had befallen their loved ones. They deserved to give them a final resting place, better than a weeded area, off a dirt road in the middle of Nowhere, Texas.

"Poor kid," I muttered under my breath, slapping my rage out on two mosquitos that landed on my forearm. Mud puddles pocked the field, which made great breeding grounds for the flying, blood-suckers; the humidity from last night's rain gave it a swamp-like vibe. Septembers could be just as hellish as summer months in Texas, sometimes worse. I cursed under my breath, scowling, as icky sweat zig-zagged down my spine. Then I scanned the horizon for carrion birds, but the sky looked clear ahead.

I shot a glance at Gary a few yards to my right. Hunched over, he looked particularly grim this morning, as he swung his pole out front, foraging through a massive clump of weeds for clues. How he organized and endured these expeditions, especially when they involved children, was beyond me. I imagined it chewed up a piece of his soul each time.

"Hey—you okay, Gare?" I asked, speaking as discreetly as I could.

Since I'd been coming out for searches most weekends, and even some weekdays when I could, we'd developed a close friendship. Gary's own experience with complex trauma, the type I'd experienced with my mom's abduction, allowed him better insight and understanding into the depth of my grief, the abysmal sadness that sometimes threatened to knock me to my knees without warning. He'd helped me through some truly dark days, and he'd also given me the name of a therapist who specialized in treating it. But I worried about him, that maybe he drank too much, that he needed to take better care of himself. His skin looked slightly jaundiced, the paunch appeared more pronounced over his belt, and the bags sagging under his eyes looked more puffy than usual, if that was possible.

He flicked his dejected baby-blues my way and nodded.

"Doin' fine, darlin'," he said, his voice flat, as he continued on, his boots sloshing through a particularly deep mud puddle without hesitation. "You holdin' up?"

"Yeah, but the mosquitos make it extra sucky today," I said, grumbling as I eyed him closely. Then I smiled at him. "Excuse the pun."

"Yep." He gave a token chuckle, folded a piece of spearmint gum in his mouth—offering me a piece out of the pack, which I declined—and kept moving, his glossy eyes sweeping the ground near his feet. "Those miserable bastards always do."

His perseverance amazed me. How he managed to keep hope that one day he'd find his son. How he kept poking his way through endless fields of knee-high weeds and mounds of rocks and dirt, never giving up faith. No doubt he'd walked thousands of miles in his search, uncovered hundreds of bodies, helped many families find closure when he could. Would I wind up like Gary, I wondered, carrying a crushing weight of sorrow on slumping shoulders, spending my life hunting for remains that I might never find, but determined to keep searching? I probably would. Like Gary, I needed to keep moving, afraid if I stood still, even for a moment, I'd somehow miss that one bit of evidence that would lead me to my mom. I couldn't take that chance.

It had been more than four months—one hundred twenty-five days, two hours and twenty-two minutes, to be exact—since I'd last seen her. I still prayed she was alive, and I remained determined to find her, but a part of me feared she'd slipped farther and farther away with each day. She still visited my dreams, but most times she didn't speak, standing off to the side in silence, her closed lips upturned wistfully. Sometimes I'd wake in near panic, afraid I'd forgotten the different sounds of her laughter, the convulsive kind she'd belt out while watching a goofy Will Ferrell comedy, or the melodic tone she'd switch to when she'd playfully say my name after trouncing me in a round of Scrabble. After those panicky moments, when I'd jackknife in bed, my heart in a wild sprint, my legs twisted in the covers, I'd force myself to retrieve favorite memories, like the time we rode a roller coaster at Six Flags, her hands white-knuckling the safety bar next to mine and laughing hysterically as we'd dropped what felt like ten stories. Or the time I had bronchitis when I was eight, hacking and crying on and off through the night, and she stayed next to me the entire time, rubbing a menthol ointment on my back and softly humming songs to lull me to rest. I'd close my eyes and sit with the sounds and images of our lives together through the years, my only home movies of the two of us, and eventually I'd settle down and breathe regularly again.

A whistle shrieked, startling me from my thoughts. I used the edge of my shirt to wipe off my dampened hairline, then grabbed a jumbo water jug from my backpack, having learned the hard way to keep myself hydrated. I waved across the way at Dee, the woman I'd been a jackass to on my first search with the group. I'd been too quick to judge her when we'd met, later learning she'd joined the team a few years back, after her sister went missing while out on a morning jog. Dee's sibling had been found beaten to death in a field similar to this one, a victim of her abusive ex-boyfriend, who'd been subsequently arrested and convicted for her murder. I'd been better to Dee since learning of her own tragedy, empathetic to her loss, and tried extra hard to make amends for my juvenile behavior.

"You still plannin' on graduating early? What—mid-December, right?" Gary asked, after a long and loud gulp from his water bottle. "You better invite me to the commencement, you hear?" He took another long draw of water, wiping his mouth with the back of his hand. "You decide about college, yet?"

"Yeah, I'll finish my final semester online—my teachers understand. It's just—it's difficult to focus when I'm at school. Plus, I can't handle classmates and teachers asking me lots of questions about her—or worse, not saying anything at all," I said, grabbing for the mosquito repellent spray in my pack. I sprayed my arms and around my ankles and rubbed a bit on my neck, ears and face. "I'm going to go through the graduation ceremony with the rest of my class in May, though, so I can walk with my debate friends, and Cici, of course."

I tossed the spray can, and he caught it with one hand.

"Looks like I'll enroll at community college next semester. Stay close to home, you know? Or maybe take a gap year, I dunno," I said, shrugging. "Who knows? Maybe I'll change my mind next fall, depending on what happens, but right now it feels good to stay put. I wanna be close to my uncle and friends."

"Yep, I get that," he said, spraying down like I did. Then he tossed the can back with an impish grin that briefly lifted his weary face. It took about ten years off his appearance when he smiled like that. "Makes me happy you'll still be around these parts, not off in some god-forsaken state like Cali, like that boyfriend of yours. Why the hell anyone would wanna live in that state kinda scrambles the brain—know what I mean?"

I chuckled, even though the thought of Luka thousands of miles away stabbed at my chest, the tiny space just above my heart. He had left for college in San Diego a month ago. I knew he had to go, but it still hurt to see him drive away for the airport. Afterwards, Cici had taken me for milkshakes and chili pies, and later we cruised around town with the music blasting. For a couple of hours, I had tried to enjoy being a typical teenager out for a joyride with her best friend, talking about songs and movies we wanted to see, and laughing about stupid stuff.

Two days later, I had turned eighteen. What should have been a happy milestone birthday for me turned out to be one of the worst. No amount of cake, flowers or gifts brought me joy, not without my mom there to share the day with me. Even endless texts from Luka, who had become my official boyfriend, couldn't make me smile. Instead, I'd cried most of the day, lost in how much I missed her. Lost in a misery of possibilities—places where she might be, dangers she could be facing, including the cancer that was probably ravaging her body without treatment. I threw one hell of a pity party that day, but not the celebration my uncle, Shilpa, and Cici had been hoping for. The next day, though, I rallied myself out of bed, went to work at the taekwondo studio, and taught children defense moves, along with how to kick the crap out of people who meant them harm. That had made me feel less helpless.

The whistle sounded, and the chain snapped to again, slowly lurching forward with each of us combing the area, inch-by-inch. I found myself wondering about the young girl who we were looking for. I wondered about Jordan's parents, whether they had any inkling their little girl had met a pervert playing a mindless video game online. I bet they hadn't suspected anything like that would ever happen. And why should they have suspected? Why couldn't a young person play a game without some creep luring and killing them? It angered me, I suppose, that the laws that regulated nature, the existence of predator and prey, had never been limited to the wild. The same natural laws had existed within civilizations since their beginnings, and long before, despite it all.

The grief, that dark energy that often visited, came to me again. It fueled me as I carefully worked my way through the field, looking for any sign that might help find her. It walked along beside me, a presence much larger and imposing than myself, commanding that I push myself harder, that I examine every blade of grass, each brittle weed. Perhaps that was Gary's secret, too. Maybe that was the deeper bond the two of us shared.

The phone buzzed in my pocket, and irritated that it broke my concentration, I paused for a quick look at the screen. I flipped to my messages, where I saw a notification. I came to an abrupt stop, as the others continued moving.

"Hey—what is it, Mireya?" Gary said, with a sideways flick of his eyes, as he picked his way past me.

"What?" I looked up at him. I'm sure my face showed a variety of emotions. Surprise. Confusion. Fear. Longing.

He stopped abruptly, too, his brow scrunched as he stepped closer. "You okay? Is it bad news? You look shaken."

Yeah. That was it. I was shook. To the core. I stared at the screen, then tried to refocus on Gary. His face had turned almost gray, as he squinted hard at me.

"Is it your mom, darlin'? Did they find something?" he asked, eerily calm, but blinking fast, his eyes watering at the inside corners.

"No. It's not Mom," I said, shaking my head, breathless. "It's my aunt—I mean my biological aunt. She just received the message I sent her a while back. You know, the ancestry site I told you about?"

"Yeah, yeah," he said, relief washing over his features, "I remember."

I looked down at my aunt's reply. *My aunt.* It sounded weird, since I'd never had one before. Her reply was long and rambling with lots of exclamation points. I scanned it, aware that others in the search group were stopping to stare at me and Gary. The gist of it was she wanted to talk to me as soon as possible. Three exclamation points after that statement. She had seen the photo I'd posted of myself on the site and knew the minute she laid eyes on my face, she'd written. She wanted to meet the niece she'd never known she had. And she wanted to know about her sister—where was she and what had happened to her?

I looked up at Gary, my stomach suddenly twisted in a knotty mess.

"How am I supposed to tell her about her sister? I don't know how to say it to her."

He stood next to me, staring at the volunteers in front of us, before turning up toward the sky. He grabbed a bandana from his back pocket, mopped at his neck, then looked my way. Sadness emanated from him, but there was also a steeliness behind his gaze.

"Listen, you'll find the words—because you have to find them. There's no other way." At that, he straightened his shoulders, and lifted his chin, regarding the endless field before us. "You'll tell her, and then you two, well, you'll move forward. That's how it's gotta be."

I pocketed my phone, and following his lead, resumed the search, continuing to comb the area just as before. Gary was right. Somehow, I'd come up with the words to explain to my aunt what had happened to her big sister. There was no choice but to find them.

CHAPTER 28

One Hundred Forty-Four Days Missing

It took close to three weeks before I gathered the courage to call my biological aunt, whose name was Deborah McCrary. She and her husband lived in an affluent beach town on the northwest coast of Florida, where they owned and operated a small advertising agency. We stared at each other on screen during the video call, both speechless on how much we looked alike. The matching curve of our cheeks, the same protruding collarbones. Similar mannerisms, and our voices shared a matching resonance. Only eight years older than me, she easily could have passed for my older sister.

"My gosh," she'd said, with a loud gulp. "You're the—spitting image of her, except for—for those remarkable eyes." Her voice broke, as she struggled to control emotions, her painted nails fluttering in front of her face. "I'm just—you even smile like her—I'm trying to wrap my brain around it. It's like—I'm seeing her again—after so many years."

I quietly studied her onscreen, trying to absorb how surreal my life had become. Like a strange *Lifetime* movie. This woman and I shared DNA, but she knew absolutely nothing about me, or vice-versa, and yet, she felt so familiar to me.

"Where is she now? We never knew what happened to her. One moment she was there, and then she was gone. And that was it," she said, dabbing at her damp face with wads of tissue. "Our parents never stopped looking for her. They hounded the police nonstop, but no one could figure out what exactly had become of her. Just another case of a missing girl with no leads."

I swallowed hard, keeping my body as still as I could. Hearing the pain in her voice, and seeing it in her face, it was difficult not to break down.

"It haunted them both for the rest of their lives—it affected all of our lives, really," she said, blowing out a ragged breath. "Mom never recovered after Michele went missing—she suffered a heart attack about ten years ago, but I personally believe she died of a broken heart. And, Dad, well, he died a few years back in that first wave of Covid."

"That's awful. I'm so sorry," I said, with a sad, longing that tinged my voice. "I would have liked meeting them—my grandparents, I mean."

"They would have loved to meet you, too," she said, a wistfulness tugging at her lips.

I had debated how to handle the situation, whether to tell her right away about what had happened to her sister or let it out little by little. It was a lot to unpack, after all, and I still grappled with the fact that my teenage, biological mother had died giving birth to me. How the hell was I supposed to explain it all? In the end, I figured I'd tell her most of what I knew, but not all—that her sister, after being abducted, had died in childbirth, and I had been raised by another victim, who had escaped their captors with me in tow. I also told her that the man who'd been responsible for their abductions faced charges for sex trafficking, among other crimes.

There were long pauses on the other end of the line, spells of silent weeping, as she digested what had happened to her sister, without me revealing gory details. Then I explained my mother's recent disappearance and its connection to the man who had taken both her and my biological mother.

"I heard about that missing teacher from Texas. It was all over the national news," she said, blowing her nose, her face a reflection of the grief on mine. "She's been missing a while, right? I had no idea there was a connection to Michele's case. But how could I have known? It's all too much—my head feels like it might explode."

She remained quiet on the other end of the line, and I didn't try to fill in the silence. She needed time.

"I'm so sorry for what you've been through," she said, when she finally spoke. "You must be an incredibly strong person. I hope they find her soon."

We talked for more than two hours. Sometimes it was intense, and other times we giggled nervously, each sharing a similar sense of humor. It was difficult to explain—weird, but strangely cool, at the same time. Deborah shared stories about my mother, bits of what she could recall from their childhood together, that her big sister was known for her kindness, something she most certainly inherited from their mom. She'd been smart, always received academic awards for good grades, and volunteered in the church youth group. One of Deborah's favorite memories was of her sister and father performing folk rock at local bars and coffee shops in Durango, Colorado, where the family had lived. My mother had played guitar with their dad, she said, the two of them singing Bob Dylan and James Taylor songs together. Hearing her speak about my biological mother made me feel closer to her, like she had been more than just a figment of a past I couldn't recollect.

As Deborah spoke, I wondered if her sister had sung folk songs to me when I was inside her belly. Had I known her voice, the first voice

I'd ever heard, and would I recognize it if I were to hear it now. My mother had been a real person, a girl who'd playfully teased her little sister—an A-plus student who'd loved to read and listen to music, a teen who'd cut up with her best friends outside the local movie theater. She had laughed often and sang loudly and loved many. She had been an exceptional person, someone I would have enjoyed hanging out with, if only I'd had the chance. Listening to my aunt describe her, it made total sense why Mom had cared about her the way she had. Why she had felt the need to protect her, as best she could, and me, by association.

"I can't tell you how much it means to me to meet you," Deborah said, before we ended our call. "I have so much more to share—not just stories, but photos and family videos, all kinds of stuff—so I hope we can figure out the next steps to see each other face-to-face. I know we need to let today sink in, and I know you don't want to leave Texas with your mom's situation still unresolved, but I can fly out for a visit with you as early as next month. You can think about it, let me know what you think."

"Actually, that would be wonderful, Ms. McCrary—"

"Please—" she interrupted, "please, call me Aunt Deborah." We both paused, blinking at one another on screen, then she gave a small shrug. "Besides my hubby, you're the only family I have left, since my folks are gone. I know circumstances have kept us from knowing each other, but I sure hope we can make up for the time that was stolen from us."

I smiled wide. "Like I was saying, it would be wonderful to see you in person, Aunt Deborah."

I knew with certainty that I'd be seeing a lot of my aunt in the years to come. I couldn't wait to introduce her to the rest of my family—Uncle Angel, Cici, Shilpa, and Luka. And I couldn't wait to continue to learn more about my birth mother and grandparents through her stories. It filled in some of the blanks for me, filling out a family tree that had been mostly empty spaces before.

CHAPTER 29

Two Hundred Ninety-Four Days Missing

I felt a series of vibrations at my collarbone, as I stood in front of a full class of young students, praising them for crushing it during their sparring sessions. I ignored the phone tucked inside my white gee under the strap of my sports bra, letting the call go to voicemail.

"I'm so stinking proud of you," I said, clapping for the children who gathered in front of me. "Those were fancy self-defense moves, my friends! Y'all killed it! And because you did so well, I'm giving you ten minutes of free time at the kick bag before your parents get here. So, go on, hurry up! And no bag hogging!"

The kids whooped with ecstatic faces, fist bumping each other, then lined up in single file to take turns sending their spindly legs full force into the large canvas bag that shimmied from the ceiling. I rarely awarded them this type of free time, hyper-diligent about teaching them all I could about defending themselves, but they'd earned it today. The vibrations immediately started again. Whoever it was really wanted to speak with me. Maybe it was one of their parents calling to say they'd be running a little late, which happened often. I pulled out the phone, noting an incoming call with a familiar name on the screen.

It wasn't a parent. It was Detective Cho. My heart skipped several beats, as it always did when I received a call from her or Detective Anderson. When we'd first met, I hadn't cared much for either one of them, but over the more than eight months that had passed, I'd realized they had been trying to help find my mom all along. At some point after the incident with Snake, I realized they weren't to blame for the lack of details surrounding her disappearance. Maybe they had a new lead in the case? Maybe there was information on Snake's upcoming trial? I fumbled to answer the call as fast as I could.

"Hello? Detective Cho? Hold on a sec," I yelled loudly into the phone, as I moved to the side of the room, shushing a few of the louder kids playing near me, so I could hear her. My students continued screaming playfully, but at lower decibels. "Sorry about that. Just finished a class. Go ahead—what did you say? I didn't catch that."

She spoke uncharacteristically soft, the words had an airy feel to them, despite what she was saying. Something about the skeleton of a woman's body that had been found in West Texas. Something about a car in a rocky pit in an obscure county I'd never heard of. Suddenly weak, I leaned against the wall, attempting to bolster myself. An oblivious kid joyfully shrieked near me, and I shuddered as the shattering sound pierced my brain. I sunk to the floor into a squatting position, the phone pressed to my ear, the wall snug against my back.

"Listen to me. We don't know for certain if it's your mother or someone else, so please try to stay calm," she said, the somberness of her voice saying she thought otherwise. "They have forensic testing in the works, but it could take weeks. I wanted you to know right away what was happening before you saw it on the news."

"I appreciate that," I said, my faint voice sounding like it was coming from a faraway place, my face half-buried in my hand. I squeezed my eyes shut. "Does my uncle know, yet?"

"Yes, we called him a few minutes ago."

"Oh, okay." I didn't know what else to say. A numbness began spreading through my body, a sensation of being partially paralyzed. My words came out shaky. "Thank you for letting me know, Detective."

"Of course," she said. "And Mireya?"

"Yeah."

"I think it's best you wait for your uncle. He's on his way right now—said he could be there in ten minutes. Will you wait for him?"

"Sure," I managed to get out, before I hung up. What if it was Mom's body they'd discovered? Was that how her story ended? It couldn't be. And, if it was, I had failed to protect her, to bring her home safely. I remained against the wall, eyes still closed, as the lively hum of students and their arriving parents filled the taekwondo studio. I heard footfalls padding closer.

"Miss Torres?" a squeaky voice interrupted my thoughts. "Excuse me, Miss Torres? My mama wants to talk to you."

I opened my eyes to find Bryan, a brown-eyed, freckled-faced ten-year-old with a missing front tooth, looking at me with a wrinkled nose. For a second, he reminded me of Gary's boy, who was the same age when he went missing. I forced myself to stand.

"You feeling bad, Miss? You look kinda funny," he said with a slight lisp, then tugged on his mother's shirt. "Doesn't she look funny, Ma?"

"Hush, Bry." His mom ruffled his hair and gave me an apologetic smile, before Bryan sprinted toward a group still lined up at the kick bag. "Hope I'm not intruding—I just wanted to thank you for this class. For what you've done to help our son. He has been struggling with a bully in his grade, but since he started your class a few months back, his self-confidence to stand up for himself—well, it's been nothing short of transformational."

I cleared my throat and managed a small smile. It was *not* a certainty. The detective said it might not be her. I had to keep moving. Had to remember that whatever had happened to my mom, and wherever she was, she'd want me to focus on the present, on the future, on the things I could change, and those whom I could help protect.

"He's one of my best students—pays attention, tries hard," I said, sliding the phone back under my taekwondo uniform, the feeling slowly returning to my limbs. "Sorry to hear about the bullying at school, though. Some kids can be jerks, but it makes me happy knowing he can stand his ground with them. I had to do the same thing when I was his age."

"Well, thank you for making a difference with him—and with all these kiddos. That's all I wanted to say to you. I know I speak for many of the parents—we really appreciate what you're doing for our children." She shook my hand, then turned to collect Bryan. I hoped she hadn't seen my lips tremble. I'd needed to hear her encouraging words at that exact moment. My mom would have called it divine intervention.

"Later, Miss Torres!" Bryan yelled over his shoulder, as he followed behind his mother, the bell on the door jingling as it closed. Only a few students ambled in the room, playing while waiting for their rides.

Seconds after the door swung closed behind Bryan and his mom, the bell jangled again. A haggard-looking Uncle Angel came through the doorway. Our eyes met, and without saying a word, we walked purposefully toward each other, and embraced. I pressed my face into the solidness of his shoulder, but I didn't sob, even though every part of my being wanted to fold over and wail. I'm guessing he probably wanted to cry, too.

But it wasn't time for tears—it was time for faith that whatever happened, everything would be alright. I had to believe that. That's what she would want from us.

CHAPTER 30

Two Hundred Ninety-Six Days Missing

E ndless miles. I had traveled so far, both figuratively and literally, to get here. My destination just minutes away. And though I wanted to see it for myself, at the same time, I longed to run from it, far from the ugly secrets it might hold. Driving at a slow speed on the narrow dirt road, dust rose in a plume of clay-colored smoke behind me. I'd been heading east for at least fifteen minutes, waist-high buffalo grasses fencing me in on either side. It was mind-numbing, the emptiness of the land out here, but I focused on navigating the road. Even the blue sky—which expanded infinitely above—seemed to press down around me.

A few times my small car threatened to bottom out, the tires catching in large ruts, its underside scraping against uneven, hard-packed earth. I pushed forward, muttering a string of curse words aloud to release my tension. In my hurry this morning, I had left my sunglasses at the hotel. A harsh afternoon light reflected off the hood, and my eyes narrowed into slits against the glare. I didn't see the road dip unexpectedly until I was right on it, the grasses to the sides transforming into rusty, rocky walls as I crept down the slope. My stomach lurched; my foot pumped the brakes every couple of feet. This was it. The caliche pit where I was supposed to meet the Dawson County sheriff's deputy in about an hour. But I had come early. If it really was her, and they seemed ninety-nine percent certain it was, I needed time alone, to see where they had brought her. There were words that needed to be spoken, even if their sound and meaning slipped unheard into the wind.

I slowed to a crawl, readjusting to the surroundings. Rocks crunched under my tires and pinged against the belly of the car. Craggy cliffs speckled with cacti and squatty bushes surrounded the pit of caliche, a white rock that was crushed and used to cover dirt roads and driveways. Before I could register it, a hairy creature, roughly the size of two bull-dogs stacked side-by-side, darted in front of me and into nearby scrub brush. But the thing wasn't any type of dog I'd ever seen.

"Holy shit!" I slammed on the brakes, fishtailing on the rocks. "What the fuck?" The dark creature had lurched in front of me, like a blurred shadow, gone before I could even focus on it. Maybe a javelina? I'd never actually seen one. Checking all sides around me, I searched for whatever the hell it was, my knuckles clamped white around the steering wheel. I couldn't see it anywhere. A hammering heartbeat blasted inside my head. So, maybe I should have gone with Uncle Angel, like he wanted, but he'd been called on an urgent assignment to break a case they'd been working for months. I would've had to wait at least a week before he was free; I didn't want to wait anymore. I also could have brought Luka with me—he had wanted to come. His flight from San Diego to Lubbock, the nearest big city out here, had arrived late last night, and this morning, he looked wrecked from no sleep. I'd snuck out of bed and quietly dressed in the hotel bathroom, careful not to wake him. I'd left a note scrawled in eyeliner on the bathroom mirror. Even though being alone made me uneasy, it was something I needed to do.

I straightened in my seat. "Get your shit together!" I barked at my reflection in the rearview mirror, then resumed my descent.

Slowing to a stop, I shut off the engine, craning my neck to take it all in. It resembled a small canyon about the size of two football fields, surrounded by walls maybe forty-feet high. A ghoulish wind whistled high above when I stepped from the car. I stood frozen. The constant wailing creeped me out. During our conversation on the phone, the deputy had told me drug runners occasionally used the abandoned pit as a transport area, flying small aircraft in from Mexico under the reach of radar. They'd land in the nearby fields and conduct business transactions concealed by these walls. I shuddered, understanding how vulnerable I was in this desolate place. How alone she must have felt. No one would have heard her screams, her cries for help. I prayed a silent prayer she hadn't been brought here and ended with a Sign of the Cross. I swallowed a moan and forced myself toward the yellow police tape that cordoned off a large section near the middle of the rock-strewn cavity. Each hair on the back of my neck rose, as I stepped nearer. Someone was watching me, tracking from above. I could feel it on my skin.

Shielding my eyes from the sun, I scanned the area. A shadowed figure moved high above. My chest squeezed, cutting my breath short. I ducked into a defensive stance, ready to make a run for my car. Maybe I shouldn't have come here without the deputy. There was nowhere to hide at the bottom of this hellhole, and if someone planned on shooting me, or whatever, I wasn't going to make it easy. The movement above continued. I squinted harder, focusing on the large shadow climbing the side of the caliche pit. It hopped up from a tiny ledge to another with uncanny agility. Like it had Spiderman moves. I couldn't believe what I saw. It was a large, bearded goat with enormous, curved horns, and a long shaggy beard. What was it doing in a caliche pit in the middle of nowhere? More movement caught my attention, and I marveled at groups of them clinging to the walls in clumps as they warily stared back at me. Theirs were eyes that had seen ungodly things. Of that, I was sure.

"I'm not here to harm you," I called up to them, as if they could understand. I extended my palms to them. Why I was talking to mountain goats, I wasn't sure, but a compulsion overtook me to tell them why I had invaded their sacred space.

"I won't stay long! I'm just looking for—Look, I'm just trying to find my mother. I need to know if—." Silent, they stared back with dark, haunted eyes. I sensed their pity—they knew who I was looking for. I wished they could speak, tell me what they had seen. But maybe I didn't need to know.

Approaching the crime scene tape, I saw the blackened frame of a car. It was covered with splotches of ashy gray, and random singed pieces of metal scattered the ground around it. Someone had set fire to it, letting it burn to the ground. My guess was whoever had done it had waited until the dead of night. No one would have spotted the raging blaze inside the pit or the curls of dark smoke snaking into inky sky. It was the perfect place to murder someone—unseen, unheard. With only stoic goats to witness the unspeakable.

"Mamí? Are you—" I whispered, choking back tears. I folded under the yellow-tape barrier, and came up on the other side, moving closer to study the scene. "Is this where they brought you? Please tell me no. Please tell me where you are." A sob escaped me. I took in the small orange flags on the ground that showed where evidence had once been. Bones, most likely, scattered by wild animals long after the fire had burned out, photographed by authorities, then bagged and boxed and taken away. The tattered markers littered the area—fifty-eight flags in all. I counted each one. Fifty-eight bones, some fragments, some whole, I figured. Remnants scattered like something unwanted, like trash. Images of what might have happened flickered in my mind's eye, pictures of her bloodied, lifeless body drenched with gasoline, the lighting of the match, the flames dancing higher and higher. *Oh God.*

I squeezed my eyes shut, the heels of my hands pushing against my temples, trying to block out the tormenting images. I felt a quickening, a rage ignited inside, consuming me, much like the flames that had surely engulfed the gutted car before me. It sucked all oxygen from my body. Helpless to do anything, I let its intensity take me over, finally erupting as I lifted my face and screamed.

"No!" My voice echoed, lonely, bouncing off canyon walls, dissipating into the air around me. "NOOOO!"

I hated this place. She had deserved better than this bleak quarry. No. My mother's last breath couldn't have been here. Or anywhere, for that matter. I refused to believe it. They were wrong. Law enforcement made mistakes all the time. They hadn't identified the car; it had no plates. And the burned woman's bones they'd discovered could belong to someone else, some nameless, faceless victim. Someone else's mother. Not mine. *Please, God, not mine.*

"You're wrong, you stupid creatures," I shouted at the goats, my fists balled against my head. "She's alive, damn you! I need to find her!"

The animals, as still as statues, blinked back in response.

"I just—. You can't be—here, Mamí," I uttered between sobs. The unnatural wind kicked up even louder above, filling the canyon with an even more unnerving howl, which drowned out my cries. Gasping, I sucked in a mouthful of dust and began coughing. I leaned over, hands on knees, working at composing myself, and ignoring the spooky sounds surrounding me, the pity-filled glances from above.

"Hey." A man's deep, gravelly voice sounded from close behind, as strong fingers grabbed my shoulder. "What the hell do you think you're—?"

Instinctively, I broke away and spun around, ready to shove the heel of my hand into his nose.

Spotting his badge, I stopped myself a millisecond before making contact. He had a forearm shielding his face and was reaching for a holstered gun. "Whoa, lady. What the—?"

He stumbled back, and slowly extended a hand in front of him, the other resting on the gun holster at his hip. The deputy's face was sunburned red, his brow furrowed tight over angry-bright gray eyes, his bottom lip puffed out with chew. He spit tobacco juice and wiped the corner of his mouth, breathing hard.

"Dammit, Miss, I get you're upset an' all, and I can't say I blame you none, but that don't give you license to contaminate a crime scene. Or attack a law enforcement officer, for that matter," he said, his voice almost a yell. "You wanna honor this investigation, right? Find the bastards that done it?"

"Yes—I'm sorry," I said, the rage leaving as I grasped the importance of his words. "I didn't hear you drive up. You scared me."

"Fine, fine. But I suggest you get back over here. That's it," he said as he gently guided me to the other side of the tape. "We'll pretend like this never happened, y' hear? What the DA don't know won't hurt her, right?"

Dazed, I nodded. The deputy ducked his head and spit again.

"I know you wanted to come here today. I'm not sure it does you any good, but I hope it helps," he said, less angry but still eyeing me with caution. He took off his hat, wiped sweat off his forehead, placing it back on top of russet-colored, thinning hair.

"Why do you think it's her?" I asked. My voice was sharp and jagged like the pieces of rock around me.

"Well, we're not a hundred percent, but the, uh, skeleton seems to fit the height and age, according to the forensic anthropologist's initial exam. And the length of time it looks to have been setting out here, along with the car, appears to fit, too." He rubbed the back of his neck. "The air out here is dry, so that's good. Helps preserve things, like the bones and all, so that'll benefit us with the investigation into what happened out here."

I stared at the ground, scraping dirt with the toe of my sneaker.

"Like I said, the forensic anthropologist, well, she hasn't filed a report yet—might take a while—but the time of the suspected, uh, death would match up about right with when your mom went missing," he said, when I didn't speak. He tapped his chin and shrugged. "But, then again, it might not be her. We're waiting on dental records and whatnot for definite confirmation."

His words filtered into my brain. Slowly. I nodded, blinking back the sting of them, then stared at the sky, at the shaggy goats, at the caliche, chalky white in the sun. Grit had settled along the back of my tongue. So many questions—but no sound left my lips. Maybe because I didn't want to know. Not the details. It hurt too much to know what they might have done to her. If it was her.

"Sir?" I asked. "Tell me the truth. You really think it's my mom?"

"I'm sorry to say, but yes, ma'am, it's lookin' like it very well could be." He stared at the ground in front of him and rocked on the heels of his scuffed cowboy boots, thumbs tucked in the belt loops of starched jeans. He cleared his throat, and looked up at me, his head leaning to one side. "Listen, I'll tell ya what. I'm gonna go sit in my truck and work on a report and whatnot. You take some time alone. When you're done, we'll head on back to the office." He walked to the cab of his pickup, calling over his shoulder, "Stay outside that tape, though, ya hear?"

Almost ten months had passed. So much had happened since the day she disappeared. I had discovered so much about her, her past, and what she had sacrificed to save me. I had learned about myself, too, and what I was capable of. I had taken on the Devil himself and left my mark. The only thing I hadn't found was her body. Where her bones had finally rested. I began walking the parameter around the crime scene.

"Mamí, are you here? I can't feel you," I murmured to the burned remains of the car, to the scrub brush under foot, to the emptiness. "I think about you every day. You need to know how much I love you." I wiped away tears. "I've memorized everything about you. The dimple on the side of your mouth when you smile, your laugh. Sometimes I hear you—" I shook my head, a small sob-laugh escaping my lips. "I know—I sound crazy, right? Not knowing where you are, it has made me insane."

I shuffled along, whispering to her, hugging myself, moving outside the taped-off area, careful of where I stepped and cognizant of rattlesnakes and scorpions that probably lived inside this pit, too.

About halfway around the perimeter, my eye caught a tiny glint of silver, so small I might have missed it if I had blinked at the wrong nanosecond. Something lay on the ground, mostly buried under a pile of caliche and dust. I squatted low and scooped it up, rubbing it on my jeans. I instantly recognized the coolness of the metal chain, the weight of it in the palm of my hand, the smooth cut of the elephant figurine that dangled from it. Brought back from India by Shilpa, it was a trinket of admiration, a token of love, a symbol of wisdom. How many times had I tried it on or adjusted it as it had encircled Mom's neck? I brought the elephant to my lips, and disregarding the chalky taste, kissed it like she had always done, like it was the crucifix attached to her rosary.

Placing the chain around my neck, I knew for certain. Rivulets of tears leaked from my eyes, but I tried to smile, for her sake more than mine. I lifted my face to the warmth of the sunlight, felt her kiss upon my lips, a long embrace, warm and firm, like the one we had shared that last morning. "I understand, Mamí." The search was over. This was her farewell. She'd intentionally dropped the necklace when they brought her here, so that I would know without a doubt. She was gone, but she'd protected what she treasured most. Me. She had protected me.

Looking around with new eyes, the desolate pit transformed into sacred ground, the horned goats now its guardians. I whispered another prayer into the wind, made the Sign of the Cross, and dragged a large, flattened rock to the spot where I had found the necklace. Next time I'd bring flowers and light candles, placing them on the makeshift altar. I'd bring Uncle Angel, Cici and Shilpa, if she would come. My mom would like that. I would come back here to honor her—our life together, the courage she showed, the love she gave—and one day I would gather my mother's bones and take them home, where they belonged.

I headed back to the car, dragging myself against the wind.

"Did you see something on the ground out there?" The deputy watched me approach his truck. "Looked like you mighta found something?"

"No, sir," I lied, then shrugged, "Just dropped my necklace. The clasp doesn't always close properly—sometimes it slides off."

"Huh." His arm dangled outside the window of his truck. He squinted hard at me, then spit into an empty Coke can in his other hand. "That right?"

"Yep. Gotta fix this thing—don't want anything to happen to it. My mother gave it to me," I said, then changed the subject, as I wiped at my tear-stained face. "So, should I follow you? I don't really know where I'm going."

"Sure thing, ma'am. I'll go slow for ya."

As I drove behind him, ascending from the bottom, leaving the caliche behind, I pressed the elephant pendant against my breastbone. Yes, I had lied, withheld evidence. But they wouldn't need the necklace. They would get a positive identification from the DNA in the bones. I needed it for another reason—for the comfort it brought knowing a piece of my mother would forever rest not only in my heart, but against it, as well.

CHAPTER 31

Epilogue

Forensic tests confirmed what I already knew. The skeletal remains found at the caliche site were indeed my mom's. We held a Celebration of Life Mass for her a few weeks back, and the turnout left me humbled. It would have floored her, too. About eight hundred people crammed into the church to honor Mom. Vans from local and national news agencies peppered the area, with stand-up reporters and television cameras stationed on the front lawn and sidewalks.

I tried to channel my mother's dignity, honoring her by sitting up as straight as I could manage in the front row, my chin lifted even as tears silently trickled down. Uncle Angel clasped my right hand, and Shilpa leaned into my left shoulder, a comforting pressure. (Shilpa's son, who had flown home to stay with her for a couple weeks, sat beside her, consoling her, as she sobbed on and off during the service.)

Aunt Deborah also attended, sitting next to Gary and Luka directly behind me, each of them reaching to gently touch my shoulder, from time to time. Mom would have taken comfort in seeing that I was surrounded by love in every direction. Always would be.

Condolence cards and personal notes were stacked high on a table outside the sanctuary. Lavish bouquets were sent from as far away as

Australia and the United Kingdom by those who had followed the news story about Mom's disappearance since the beginning. The inside of the church looked like a florist shop, colorful flowers everywhere.

The service was beautiful, really. I couldn't have imagined a more fitting send-off for her. Former students shared tearful stories of how my mom had kept them towing the line, how she'd inspired them to aim higher, whatever their pursuits. Average was never good enough for her, most said in their tributes, explaining that Ms. Torres had demanded their absolute best, because she'd believed in them. At the end, two of her former students—one a singer, the other a keyboardist—performed "The Parting Glass," a traditional, bittersweet Scottish song that left most of us in tears. It was perfect—she would have loved every moment. Despite facing tragic circumstances as a teen, my mom had shed a victim's skin, had paved her own path, had inspired and made a difference for others, and had been loved deeply when she departed this world. I couldn't have been prouder to be her daughter, the one she had protected at all costs.

Even in death, she continued to take care of me. She had acquired a hefty life insurance policy about ten years back, another secret she'd kept, and as her beneficiary, the funds would pay for my education and help me get established in the future. I wouldn't touch the blood money she'd squirreled away from Snake, who along with drug and trafficking offenses, had been charged with her murder. (Once an accomplice had flipped on him for a plea deal with law enforcement, he had no chance of wriggling out of it. Snake would spend his life in prison.) I couldn't risk involving Uncle Angel with any of the go-bag stash I'd found hidden, so instead of reporting it, I'd been sending large, anonymous cash donations to groups that helped survivors of sex trafficking crimes, something I'll continue doing until the last of it is gone. I figure that dirty money needs a rebirth, so to speak—a transformation from ugly into something potentially beautiful.

In the fall, I plan to transfer to the University of Texas at Austin, where Cici has also been accepted. We'll be roomies. Luka was disappointed I hadn't applied to the University of San Diego, but maybe I can convince him to go to law school in Texas in a few years. Anyway, I plan to fly out to visit him as often as I can. I chose to stay close enough to home that I could jump in the car and visit Uncle Angel, Shilpa and Gary, whenever I want. Quite honestly, when the time comes, it will take everything I have to leave them, even if it is only three hours away. We've journeyed through so much together. They are my circle, my people, my family.

Lately, I've been thinking about earning a degree in psychology or sociology, with a minor in art. Working specifically with young victims of sex trafficking appeals to me, maybe incorporating art therapy to help them work through their trauma. My mom would have liked that, I think.

I've come to realize that my mother hadn't needed me to protect her; she needed me to trust that I could protect myself. That was the treasure she'd gifted me. I often find myself thinking about Mom, whose real name I still haven't determined and whose biological family I hope someday to find using DNA. (Aunt Deborah and I also hope genetic testing will help close the cold case on my biological mother—that somewhere there's a trace, maybe discarded bones left behind that would tie her death to Snake and end the mystery of her disappearance that started so long ago. It's a long shot, but with any luck, he'll pay for her death, too.)

I've never found the thumb drive that Snake said my mom used to blackmail him. It's not for lack of trying, though. I tore up most of the baseboards in our home, desperate to locate it, hoping it would have more evidence to further fry his ass. But it wasn't there. Knowing my mom, she had bluffed him—it probably never existed. She was a master at bluffing, something my uncle and I often witnessed at our family poker games, and that skill seemed to serve her well, given what she had faced in her life.

As for me, I'm trying to soldier on like she would want, but God, there are moments that I miss her so much, times I feel a tearing sensation in my chest, like a hand reaching inside and physically ripping out my heart. Those are the days I cling to my people or work a jigsaw puzzle or light a candle at church. I might hurt in those moments, but eventually I pick myself up and move forward, the lesson she'd imparted upon me my entire life. She'd taught me resilience. And, someday, if I'm ever lucky enough to have a daughter of my own, I'll pass that gift to her.

Sometimes, I close my eyes and see those orange flags marking the spots where skeletal remains had been haphazardly scattered around the caliche pit. And I catch myself smiling grimly, because I know she had beaten Snake at his own game, even though she had died in the process. It gave me a huge amount of satisfaction knowing that those remains—what had been left of her, like the discarded carcass of an animal—are what ultimately fell a viscous predator, just as surely as if she'd shoved a spear through his heart. She had taken him down, plain and simple.

Archeologists believe bones reveal the stories of the people who left them behind. I'm not sure I buy into that entirely. Perhaps they offer a glimpse into their owners. But would the bones strewn at the bottom of that pit tell the full story of a woman who had never given birth, but who had become the best mother a girl could ever have? Could scientists who dug deep inside the bones, peering closely at the meaty parts within, the marrow, deduce that this woman had made the best chocolate-chip pancakes on Saturday mornings; had given the softest hugs without hesitation; had taken in an orphaned baby girl and taught her to stand and fight when she would need it most? Would they illustrate that she'd be missed by so many, but by one in particular? Every. Single. Day.

No—the bones would never share all, could never truly pierce the soft underbellies and thick skins that contained the souls of the creatures to which they'd once belonged. Those are the secrets buried beyond the skeletal scraps—wisps of proteins and minerals—carelessly cast away in fields, or rivers, or rocky pits, all but forgotten. But the actual essence of someone? There lies the true bounty, the treasure never to be possessed by the ones who've taken without regard—the ones who never had claim to begin with.

Acknowledgements

The characters and the specific scenarios described in *More Than Ivory* are fictional, and any errors in this book are my own. My heart goes out to the real families searching for missing loved ones targeted by predators, and for the victims trapped into human trafficking. May they all find their way home.

I am deeply grateful to my late father, Joe, who died from Covid in 2020. In his prime, he was a fourth-degree black belt and a part-time taekwondo instructor. He often cautioned me in my youth, "It's a jungle out there," and showed me how to protect myself, even though I didn't always follow instruction. (Sorry I was a difficult taekwondo student, Dad, but I hope you know I took your lessons to heart.) Special thanks to my mom, Jane, who died seven months after him in 2021. She encouraged me as a young girl to chase my dreams, and she also shared with me her love for elephants. They're intelligent, amazing family-focused creatures that deserve our respect and protection—as Ana María said, they're "so much more than ivory." I wish both my parents were here to see this book in its final form, but I have a gut feeling they're nearby. I've felt their presence many times throughout the process.

To Michele Jeter, my partner in crime since 1983, thanks for reading, re-reading, and then reading AGAIN, as this manuscript evolved. Your belief in me was a constant. Thanks for keeping up with my ADHD brain, making me laugh when I needed it, and humoring me, as I talked plot or dove down rabbit holes while researching elements of the novel. Same goes for Deborah Alvarenga, part of The Three Amigos. Thanks for reading, commenting, and sharing your enthusiasm for this story. I'm thankful to know such strong women, and I treasure our lifelong friendships.

A special shoutout to my peeps from SMU's The Writer's Path, who helped spur me along on my writing journey—especially the talented authors Suzanne Frank and Amanda Arista, aka. goddesses of the Hero's Journey. What a fantastic experience to have had as a writer and what wonderful friends I made in the program, which unfortunately ended a few years back. I miss the ol' Writer's Path posse, including Stephanie Chambers, Rick Hynes, Dawn Tufenkjian Capitel, Justin Moore, and Kristin Cicciarelli.

Special thanks to Maureen Davis, an amazing writer and friend, who critiqued early chapters and discussed characters, plot, and solutions to the world's problems over countless cups of coffee. I miss our writing group; your initial feedback was essential in the creation of this novel. Thank you, thank you, thank you.

I have so much gratitude for my buddy, author extraordinaire Heather Harper Ellett. Our chat sessions helped me through some dark days while working on this book. Whether it was gathering at a parking lot during the pandemic (at a safe distance, of course) or consoling each other through grief after losing loved ones to Covid, you managed to brighten my day. Thanks for the belly laughs when needed and the constant support. I'm extremely thankful we landed seats next to each other on that plane to NYC for The Writer's Path seminar. I treasure our friendship.

To the talented author Mindy McGinnis, your novels are gritty and inspiring. I'm grateful I connected with you through your website. Many thanks for your insightful comments and tough edits. They helped me polish this novel and get it ready for publication.

A heartfelt thanks goes to my group of exceptional beta readers/editors, including Eme Augustini, Robin Best, Anna Cox, Jean Yaeger, and Lailah Reyes. This group—a dream team of intelligent women—assisted in strengthening Mireya's story. Truly, I can't thank you enough for taking the time to read it and for your valuable feedback.

Much thanks to Adam Arista for sharing his expertise on police procedure with me. And a special thanks to Brooke Carlock for the stunning book cover design. I'm obsessed!

A shoutout to all my cheerleaders: Tammy Bird, sister; David Augustini, nephew; my Augustini-Best-Moses-Herrera-Howard-Flores extended family members; dear friends Julie Nichols, Amy McLarty, Sonia Moore, Yamil Berard, Donna Ericson, Candice Clark, Chloe Zonis, Sarah McFarlane, and Emma Adams; my Cook Children's Medical Center peeps, Laura Van Hoosier, Kim Brown, and Jeff Calaway; and cousins Jonathan and Destinee Reynolds. Thanks for believing in me as a writer. I appreciate each of you for nudging me along, whether you realized it, with encouragement when I discussed this novel.

As evidenced by the numerous folks I've listed (fingers crossed I've remembered everyone), it takes a village to write a novel—at least it does for me. Endless thanks to my husband, Kent, who read/edited/proofed at least 10 versions of this story, even though YA isn't really his thing. This novel wouldn't have happened without you. Your constant reassurance that I should stay the course has meant everything. Thank you for your patience during the many times I lost myself within the chapters of this book. And same to my gifted daughter, Annelise, who cheered me on since I began novel-writing ten years ago. *More Than Ivory* is for the two of you—the greatest loves of my life and the treasures I hold most dear.